I0589063

FINAL SOLUTION

A Soul-Searing Novella By

Dale A. Berryhill
& Kevin P. Henry

With an afterword by
Douglas Cupples, Ph.D.

DAB BOOKS

DAB BOOKS

Published through IngramSpark
www.IngramSpark.com

Depictions of real historical people in this story are fictional. All other characters are the invention of the authors, and any resemblance to any person, living or dead, is purely coincidental.

ISBN 978-0-9883596-0-4
eBook ISBN 978-0-9883596-1-1

Printed and bound in the United States of America
FIRST EDITION

Book Design
Cover design concept by Dale A. Berryhill / Graphics by Jessa Wilcoxen
Interior design and layout by Jessa Wilcoxen

Front Cover Illustration
The slave ship graphic was adapted from "Stowage of the British Slave Ship 'Brookes' Under the Regulated Slave Trade Act of 1788," a 1788 broadside published by the Plymouth Chapter of the Society for Effecting the Abolition of the Slave Trade, Plymouth, England. Library of Congress Rare Book and Special Collections Division.

The bullet graphic was adapted from an image in *Small Arms and Ammunition in the United States Service, 1776-1865*, a 1960 book published by the Smithsonian Institute.

To our moms,
"the better angels of our natures"

So long as the people do not care to exercise their freedom, those who wish to tyrannize will do so; for tyrants are active and ardent, and will devote themselves in the name of any number of gods, religious and otherwise, to put shackles upon sleeping men.

~ Voltairine de Cleyre, 1908

CONTENTS

AFTERWORDS

One

THE REQUEST

IGHTY-YEAR-OLD THOMAS HENSHAW had almost finished preparing supper when he heard his grandson at the front door. "Come on in, John," he called from the kitchen. "Have a seat. Dinner will be ready in a few minutes."

"Okay, Grandpa." John loosened his tie and stood looking around his grandfather's living room. Coming here always brought back a flood of childhood memories. The 19th-century furnishings seemed old-fashioned now in 1924, but they had formed a wonderland when he and his siblings played around them in their earliest years. The soft glow of the kerosene lamps may have been replaced by new-fangled electric lights, but the musky smell of the place still reminded him of Christmas mornings, and of his grandmother.

The elder Henshaw shuffled in, leaning on his cane with every step. John remembered when his grandfather didn't need a cane, when his old war wound didn't keep him from chasing the grandkids around the house.

"The potatoes need a few more minutes," Thomas said. He motioned for his grandson to have a seat and then dropped carefully into his own chair. As usual, he got right to the point. "When I asked you to come over without Liz and the kids, I'm sure you thought I wanted to revise my will or something. I do need your help, but it's not legal work. I assume you have to be a pretty good writer to be an attorney, don't you?"

"Well, I'm not sure how good I am, but yes, we do a lot of writing in my profession."

"Good. I need someone to help write my story. How much have I told you about my service in the Civil War?"

"Not much," John said. "Just that you enlisted at eighteen, got shot in the leg in your first skirmish, and spent the rest of the war doing clerical work."

"Actually, I enlisted three months before I turned eighteen. And I'm afraid I haven't told you the whole story."

"Oh?"

"I couldn't. They made me swear. But I reckon there's nothing they can do to me now."

"They? They who?"

"The Yankee soldiers. The government. They made me sign an oath, and they said they'd have me executed if I ever told."

"Executed? If you ever told what?"

Thomas started to reply, then paused. He was about to disclose something he had carried in silence for sixty years.

"I was involved in a secret program during the last year of the war. It was covered up by the government, for good reason. No one has heard about it to this day."

"Okay," John said, not sure what to think. "And now you want to write it down?"

"Not just write it down; I want it published. I want to write it as an article for the magazines and newspapers. It will be long enough to be serialized into two or three parts, so it will take some time, and I know how busy you are. Will you promise to tell me if you don't have time to do it?"

"Don't worry about that, Grandpa. I'd be happy to help."

Thomas smiled.

"Thank you," he said. Then he noticed a slightly melancholy look on his grandson's face. He shook his head and smiled again. "I'm not doing this because I'm about to die. My health is fine. Or as fine as it can be at eighty."

John, embarrassed that his thoughts had shown, smiled sheepishly in return.

"I'm doing this because of everything that's going on right now. I think my story might help wake people up and bring an end to some of the turmoil. You'll understand once you've heard it."

"I'm sure I will, but what turmoil are you talking about? We're in the middle of a prosperity boom."

Thomas looked at his grandson for a moment and then sighed. He stood up with difficulty, waving off John's offer of help. He limped to a table stacked with periodicals.

"You probably don't pay attention to these things like I do," he said. "Again, you'll understand why I do when you've heard my story."

As he talked, Thomas pulled out publications and dropped them on his grandson's lap. On the cover of a magazine was a black-and-white photograph of thousands of hooded Klansmen marching in formation past the Capitol Building in Washington. A newspaper carried a graphic photo of two black men strung up under a tree while a gleeful crowd of whites, including women and children, smiled at the camera. Thomas handed him several other periodicals with similar photographs and articles.

"Five years ago, when whites returned from the World War and found their jobs taken by blacks, race riots broke out in more than three dozen cities. They called it the 'Red Summer' of 1919. I know you were in law school at the time and had a new baby, but surely you remember."

"Of course. We even discussed it in my class on labor law."

"Then you'll recall that most of the riots were not here in the South," Thomas said, dropping back into his seat. "Two of the worst were in Chicago and Washington, and there were also mob attacks on blacks in Connecticut, Maryland, Pennsylvania, New York, Arizona, Nebraska. Two years later, in 1921, there was a race riot in Tulsa in which whites dropped fire bombs on black neighborhoods from biplanes. Ten thousand people were left homeless, six thousand people were arrested, and nearly a thousand were hospitalized. It's thought that more than three hundred blacks were killed, although the 'official' death toll was one-tenth of that."

"I didn't know about the biplanes. That's awful."

"Last year, the black community of Rosewood, Florida was burned to the ground by whites, who killed at least six people. I expect we'll be hearing about the next one any day now. These are not just isolated incidences. The Ku Klux Klan now has five million members, the most ever. The KKK is as popular in northern states like Indiana as it is in the South, by the way. And Jim Crow laws aren't just in the Deep South, either. I'm sure you studied Baltimore's attempt in 1910 to designate boundaries within which blacks had to live."

"Yes, we studied that. It was declared unconstitutional by the U. S. Supreme Court."

"Meanwhile, the lynching of blacks is rampant. For a while after the Civil War, during the frontier days of the West, more whites were lynched than blacks. But now that the country's been 'civilized,' the lynching of whites is approaching zero, while blacks are still lynched on a regular basis. And blacks are being lynched for the smallest of crimes, or only on suspicion of having committed a crime, and almost no one is prosecuted. You can see in that newspaper photograph that no one's worried about having their picture taken."

"Yes, I see," John said. "And I'm sorry this upsets you so much. I didn't realize you were so concerned about the Coloreds."

Once again Thomas paused, struck by his grandson's nonchalance. He realized with another sigh that this attitude was probably typical.

"I'm not concerned about the Coloreds *per se*," he said. "I'm concerned about my country. This nation almost tore itself apart over the slavery issue, and here we are sixty years later still being torn apart by the same racial tensions." He paused and looked off into the distance. "I knew a man who predicted all of this. And his prediction is coming true."

John waited patiently for his grandfather to come back to the present.

"Anyway, I have a story to tell, and it will shock people. Maybe it will shock some sense into people. Maybe it will get people thinking about what they're doing. Maybe it will change things."

"And you want me to help you write it."

"Yes, but like I said, you don't have to if you don't have time. I thought I would tell you my story over dinner and let you decide."

"Fair enough," John said.

"Good. It should be ready by now. Help me put it on."

As John dished food into his grandmother's old serving bowls, he watched his grandfather carry dishes with one hand while leaning on his cane with the other. He was tempted to ask yet again if they could get him some domestic help, but he already knew the answer.

When the table was set, the men took their seats.

"Let's say grace, then I'll tell you my story," Thomas said.

With his head bowed, John waited impatiently while his grandfather gave thanks. He smiled to himself as he remembered sitting at that same table as a small child, equally impatient for the praying to end and the eating to begin. At least this time he had an excuse for his impatience. He joined his grandfather in saying "Amen," then they started to serve themselves.

"Okay, so what kind of 'secret program' was this? And why were they going to execute you?"

"Well, I want you to understand it's not something I'm proud of. But I was twenty years old at the time, and of course it wasn't up to me. It seemed to be the right thing to do. We were at war, and things were not going well for the Confederacy. Lee's defeat at Gettysburg, in July of 1863, had been a demoralizing disaster. Vicksburg was surrendered the very next day, giving the North control of the Mississippi River all the way down to the Gulf. Not only did that give the Yankees a beachhead all along the western border of Mississippi, it also cut the Confederacy off from Louisiana, Arkansas, and Texas. When Union troops captured Knoxville and Chattanooga several months later, they solidified control of Tennessee, the first Confederate state to fall. They also solidified control of the Tennessee River, giving them two routes right into the Confederate heartland.

"By the start of '64, it wasn't hard to see that we might lose the war. Contingency plans were needed, but the Confederate leadership refused to acknowledge the reality of the situation. In fact, a whole year later, less than two months before Lee's surrender at Appomattox, Lincoln met personally with Confederate officials, but they wouldn't negotiate any kind of compromise. Even at that late date, they still demanded total independence for the South. Lincoln even offered compensation to slave owners, but they turned him down." He shook his head in disbelief.

"Didn't they know they were about to lose the war?"

"They were delusional," Thomas said with disgust. "Only one man had the courage to openly discuss our true position, and that was my commanding officer, Lieutenant Colonel Troy McFall. He wasn't just my C. O., he was my direct boss—I was his aide. In the spring of 1864, one year before the war ended, he had me hand deliver invitations to seven other military officers there at the Confederate capital in Richmond. The invitations were to an early morning meeting at the State Capitol Building, where he laid out his plans for a secret program. If the program had worked, it would have changed the course of American history. And damned us all to hell."

Two

THE MEETING

TWENTY-YEAR-OLD TOMMY HENSHAW stepped out of the Richmond boarding house and was surprised to find it was the first warm day of spring. He paused and took a deep breath of the sweet-smelling Virginia air. For a moment he was transported back to his childhood on the farm, when life was peaceful and he was in touch with the seasons. Those days seemed like a lifetime ago, even though he had enlisted in the Confederate Army only two and a half years before.

He shook his head to clear these thoughts away. He had no time for reminiscing—he was running late. He stepped carefully down from the porch and began walking the four blocks to the State Capitol Building. He walked with a noticeable limp, but it barely slowed him down. The few civilians on the street at this early hour nodded and smiled out of respect for his uniform.

At the Capitol, he saw no one except the sentries until he entered the basement conference room. The seven officers they had invited to the meeting, each from a different administrative department within the Army, were already seated around the large oak conference table. Tommy was relieved to see that his boss was not yet there.

He dropped into his seat just as Lieutenant Colonel Troy McFall strode into the room. All conversation ceased and all eyes followed him to the head of the table. McFall was handsome and charismatic. A professor of military history at West Point prior to the war, he spoke with the authority of a teacher and the confidence of one who always comes to his lectures fully prepared. He started talking before he reached his spot at the head of the table.

"Gentlemen, we have a problem. I've spoken with each of you about this problem, and I know we all agree. Today I'm going to propose a solution to this problem. It is not a particularly agreeable solution, but I believe it to be necessary. Before we begin, I would like to make several important points. These are for your own protection:

"First, this is not a meeting, but a presentation. I will simply lay out my plan, then we will adjourn. There will be no discussion. That way, if asked about it later, you can truthfully say that you did not participate in any discussion on this topic.

"Second, I am not asking you to participate in my plan in any way. My aide and I can administer this program. The only thing I need from you is the cooperation of your department.

"Third, in order for my plan to work, it must be kept absolutely confidential. What I am about to propose to you must be known only to those of us in this room. If you decide that you do not want to cooperate, you will not be required to do so. However, I must have your word before I start that you will speak of this to no one. If you cannot give your solemn pledge as a Christian gentleman, I ask you to leave now."

McFall looked around the table, ending with Tommy. He saw that Tommy, as usual, had opened his binder to take notes. McFall pointed at the binder with two fingers and moved his hand in a little arc to signal that he wanted it closed. Tommy could tell what he wanted as soon as he pointed, so he used his thumb beneath the binder to close it almost simultaneously with the colonel's motion. To those down the table, it must have looked as if McFall had closed the binder with a magical gesture.

McFall turned his attention back to his audience. "Let me begin by making this clear: We are not defeatists. We are not giving up on this war, and we will never give up. But as leaders of the sovereign nation of the Confederate States of America, it is our duty to make proper preparation for any eventuality. And there is one eventuality that the civil leadership on both sides of this conflict seems to be ignoring."

With this, Colonel McFall took his seat.

"Here it is in a nutshell: According to the 1860 Census, there are around 4,250,000 slaves in the Southern states, and only around eleven million free whites. In many rural counties, Negroes are in the majority, and they certainly outnumber their white overseers on the larger farms and plantations. If the South loses, these slaves will be freed. According to Lincoln's Emancipation Proclamation, they're already free."

McFall rolled his eyes as he said this, and a spontaneous chuckle went around the room. But before the laughter died out, he grew serious again.

"Yes, we could laugh when he issued his Proclamation, but now it's clear that the slaves in Tennessee will be freed even if we win the war. The slaves in New Orleans, the largest city in the Confederacy, are already free. So are the slaves in Baton Rouge, Vicksburg, Norfolk, and Jacksonville. Hundreds of thousands have already been freed in areas controlled by Union forces, and more are being freed with every mile the Yankees take."

He paused, looking from man to man. The room had grown silent, the reality of the situation impressing itself upon the participants. Tommy marveled at McFall's command of his audience.

"But while more slaves are being freed every day, no one seems to be asking about the practical outcomes of this freedom, for both blacks and whites. Think about it—more than four million people, uneducated, penniless, and landless, being suddenly set free. Where will they go? Where will they live? How will they earn a living? Let's look at the options:

"Will Lincoln send these freed slaves back to their African homeland? The American Colonization Society has been trying to do that since 1820. They even founded the Republic of Liberia in West Africa with freed American slaves. But in forty years, they have repatriated only around ten thousand blacks. Lincoln himself has tried to colonize free blacks elsewhere, without success. His attempt to send some to South America failed because of corruption within his administration, and when he sent several hundred freedmen to Haiti last year, the whole thing was so poorly managed that they had to be rescued by the U. S. Navy. What an embarrassment. So that option's out.

"Will the Yankees welcome the slaves they free to jobs in the North? Hardly. In most Northern states, free blacks can't vote, can't serve on juries, can't file a lawsuit, and can't testify against a white. They're limited to unskilled labor so they don't compete with white workers, and of course they're not allowed to live in white neighborhoods. Exclusion laws force blacks to register when they enter a town, limit the time they can stay, or keep them out altogether.

"Northern blacks are often the target of white violence, such as the riot in New York City in 1834 that leveled several hundred black homes. We can tell things haven't changed by the riots in New York last July. What started as a draft riot turned into a race riot that went on for several days, with hundreds of blacks lynched or just murdered outright.

"The sensible Northerners who opposed this misguided war had a cute little slogan, 'No Blood for Cotton.' But when Lincoln issued his Proclamation and then implemented the draft, the cries turned to 'No Blood for Niggers' and the lynchings followed. That's the hypocrisy of the North—so quick to dictate race relations to others when they can't keep their own house in order. In any case, inviting the freed slaves north would not be a politically acceptable option for Lincoln.

"Will the Yankees ship the freed slaves out West, where there's plenty of unclaimed land? That's what they should do, but they won't, and for one simple reason: White men want that land. They're still in the process of driving the Indians off that land; they're certainly not going to turn around and give it to the blacks. When the so-called 'Free-Soilers' of Kansas set up their territorial government, they immediately passed laws prohibiting blacks— free or slave—from entering the territory. The Oregon territory had black exclusion laws, and the Oregon state constitution, approved by voters just three years before this war started, bans all Negroes. Even David Wilmot, author of the famed Wilmot Proviso, made it clear that his motivation for prohibiting slavery in the territories was to save the land and the jobs for white settlers.

"So, the freed slaves won't be sent back home, won't be welcome in the North, and won't be allowed to move West. With those three options closed, have you heard Lincoln or anyone else discuss a plan—any plan at all—for taking care of the more than four million people they are about to set free? No, you haven't. And do you want to know why?"

Those whose eyes had wandered turned back to McFall.

"Because they don't have one. Lincoln's Republicans have launched a war without adequate preparations for securing the peace. They're in the process of freeing more than four million people and taking away their livelihood with absolutely no plan for providing for them. When slaves are liberated by Yankee troops, they're turning into camp followers, scavengers. So I ask again, where will they go when this war is over? Where will they live? How will they eat?

"I think we all know the answer. Yankee soldiers will take Southern land from the white man and give it to blacks. What other option do they have? To enforce this new world order, Union troops will occupy the South for years. Blacks will be put into positions of power over their former masters, and they will use those positions to seek revenge of the worst sort. White families won't be safe in their own homes. The world will be turned upside down.

"Want proof? Just look at what happened during the slave revolt in Haiti. Thousands of whites killed, women raped, homes burned. All the land owned by whites confiscated. And the final result? The French who had colonized Haiti were driven from its shores and the entire nation turned over to the blacks. Mind you, these were not the original inhabitants of the island driving off invaders; these were African slaves with no more claim to that land than the whites.

"If you don't think the exact same thing can happen here in the South, consider this: After Haiti gained its independence, their new constitution stated that only blacks could be citizens, and that only blacks could own land. The U. S. Constitution contains no such racial delineation, and lots of free blacks own land in America. For almost sixty years, the United States refused to acknowledge the racist Haitian government, established in violation of all human rights and international law. Thomas Jefferson imposed an embargo on Haitian goods that lasted until last year.

"And what happened last year? Why, our good friend Abraham Lincoln defied long-established policy and recognized Haiti's standing as an independent nation. He has spoken out against America's failure to treat blacks as equals, but he has no problem with a nation that massacred its white population and grants citizenship only to blacks. Can anyone blame us for assuming he'll allow the same thing to happen here?"

The men all shook their heads, their visages uniformly dark.

"Of course, the Haitian revolt inspired similar actions in America. Denmark Vesey's plan to slaughter whites in and around Charleston was foiled only because word leaked out. Nat Turner was more successful, leading a slave rebellion here in Virginia in which fifty or sixty whites, including women and children, were bludgeoned and hacked to death before the murderers were apprehended. What's to stop the slaves from enacting similar revenge all over the South the minute they're freed? If we lose, we will be disarmed, and there will be no one standing between them and us but Yankee soldiers. When that happens, do you think the Yankees will protect us?"

One man let out a snort of derision. Everyone shook their heads.

"Not only will the Yankees not protect us, they'll be in on it. We know this from John Brown's raid on Harper's Ferry, second only to Nat Turner as the largest act of domestic terrorism in American history. Brown operated with the moral and financial support of Northern abolitionists, who bankrolled his original armament of two hundred rifles and a thousand iron pikes. Their plan was to liberate slaves as they moved through the South, arming them with the iron pikes so they could stab and bludgeon whites to death before destroying their property. The people behind this plot were civilians, you understand, acting with no government authority whatsoever, planning a bloody slaughter of their own countrymen. These are maniacs who favor the freedom of blacks over the very lives of whites, and yet they don't understand why we want to leave and form our own country.

"After John Brown's raid, the Northern Democrats who opposed the war were not afraid to place blame where it belongs. They said Brown's violence was a direct result of the heated rhetoric and intolerant policies of the Republican Party. They said it was the efforts by Republicans to impose their moral and religious views on others that emboldened religious fanatics like Brown to violence. They said the Republicans should be held accountable for the violence caused by the hate they spew, and they were right.

"But what was the response to Brown's brutality among Northern liberals? The men who condemn the cruelty of slavery

had nothing but praise for this terrorist, from the abolitionist
newspapers to poets such as Henry David Thoreau. Ralph Waldo
Emerson even said that Brown would 'make the gallows glorious
like the Cross.' Can you imagine? These people say they hate man's
inhumanity to man, but they liken an attempted mass murderer to
Jesus Christ himself. These people think a violent slave rebellion
to be wholly justified, but somehow our own rebellion makes us
traitors worthy of death. In their minds, we're condemned either
way.

"They are explicit about this. Ohio Congressman Joshua
Giddings, a founding member of the Republican Party, said he
looked forward to the day 'when the torch of the incendiary shall
light up the towns and cities of the South.' The so-called
'Reverend' Theodore Parker encouraged awakening 'the fire of
vengeance' in the slaves, saying it could only be extinguished
by 'the white man's blood.' The so-called 'Reverend' George B.
Cheever said it is 'infinitely better that 300,000 slaveholders were
abolished, struck out of existence,' than for slavery to continue.
The Boston Post said that if John Brown was a lunatic, 'then one-
fourth of the people of Massachusetts are madmen.' Well, we
certainly won't argue with that, will we?"

The men around the table smiled bitterly.

"We were being openly threatened with physical annihilation
by our own countrymen—a threat they have since put into
horrendous effect—and yet we're traitors for wanting to leave?
Who are these people, who put themselves in the place of God,
dictating how we must live and pronouncing divine justice on us
if we do not obey?"

McFall's voice was rising with emotion.

"Stoked with evangelical zeal and blinded by exaggerated images of slave master cruelty from cheap novels and sensationalized news accounts, they have grown to hate us. They don't just want to free the slaves; they want revenge, and they want the slaves to have theirs. They will confiscate the South as the spoils of war, turning it over to the slaves as their 'just reward.' Then they will turn a blind eye while we, our wives, and our children are massacred—just as they were in Haiti, and just as John Brown tried to do here. Do you doubt that for a moment?"

Once again the men all shook their heads, their expressions a mixture of anger and despair.

"In fact, they are already preparing for this. When slaves are freed, they are being armed against us. Lincoln specifically called for the arming of freed slaves in his Emancipation Proclamation. In doing so, he has made every male slave a potential enemy combatant.

"Now, I ask you, what does Lincoln expect us to do in this situation? We have millions of male slaves of fighting age under our control. Are we really supposed to sit here and wait for them to be freed and armed against us? What country, what military, would be foolish enough to allow that to happen? Preventing this is clearly a top military priority. It is something we simply must do. Does anyone disagree with that?"

All heads shook in unison.

"The actions we are about to take, we take out of military necessity. And it is a military necessity created by Abraham Lincoln himself. We're doing all we can to stop the Yankees from gaining ground, but what is our plan for when they do gain ground? I can only think of one."

Once again, everyone at the table turned to look at him.

"Gentlemen, there is only one way to avoid this nightmarish fate, and that is to dispose of the problem. The only way to protect ourselves from the revenge of the Negro is to eliminate the Negro. To eradicate him from the face of the earth. I'm afraid we have no choice. Mass executions must begin immediately."

Three

——————

JUSTIFICATION

TOMMY, OF COURSE, WAS PREPARED for McFall's shocking pronouncement—he knew the purpose of the meeting. In fact, his boss had been discussing these concerns with him for weeks, slowly leading him to the conclusion that this dreadful course of action was not only unavoidable, but completely justified. He did, however, expect to hear expressions of dismay from the men around the table, and he was surprised when none came.

Leaning forward and looking down the two rows of faces, he saw each man reacting differently, but silently. No one looked happy, but no one said anything. It was almost as if they had also been expecting McFall's horrifying proposal. Then Tommy thought back over McFall's interaction with these men during the past weeks—hushed meetings behind closed doors, private lunches away from the office, whispered conversations in the hallway. While McFall had been laying the groundwork with Tommy, he had been doing the same with the rest of these men.

He had done his job well. If a single man had protested at that moment, others might have joined him. If a single man had stood up and walked out, it would have raised the threat of exposure and stopped the program before it started. Instead, the silence of each man, in the face of such a startling declaration, suggested to every other man that they were in agreement. And now that they had acquiesced, they were all in it together.

That was the real reason for this meeting, Tommy thought. McFall could have gotten each man's agreement individually and discretely, but it would have been a tenuous and secret agreement. Now, having given their silent consent in the presence of their fellow officers, they were accomplices.

For several tense yet silent moments, McFall waited, allowing the men to search their minds for alternatives, knowing they would find none. Tommy marveled at the self-control it must be taking to wait so long, risking every second that someone might speak up. Then, into the silence, McFall let out a loud sigh that brought everyone's attention back to him.

As they turned, they saw him standing up slowly, his head hung low and his face shrouded in sadness. He leaned his body on the table in front of him, his arms extended and his hands in fists on the table. He lifted his head and looked his audience in the eye. He spoke quietly and calmly, but with a tone of sadness in his voice.

"You all know me, and you know that I have never owned a slave. Neither do most of you. My young aide here also comes from a non-slaveholding family." He nodded toward Tommy. "Only one-fourth of Southerners own slaves, and nine out of ten slaveholders own twenty or fewer," he said, sounding like the professor he was.

"Like most Southerners, I don't really care whether slavery continues, and I'm certainly not fighting this war to protect the interests of the moneybags plantation owners. Given the chance,

I'd probably vote to end slavery right now, provided, of course, that the slaveholders are compensated and the freed slaves are relocated. Ending slavery wouldn't bother me one bit, but it has to be done legally, and it has to be done honestly. The abolitionists have done neither.

"The Constitution of the United States specifically provides for slavery. It's written into the contract that created the United States. If the abolitionists wanted to get rid of slavery, all they had to do was amend the Constitution. That was their one and only legal option. England outlawed slavery thirty years ago, and they did so through the democratic process. The abolitionists in England had enough faith in their views to stick to the legal process. Instead of using illegal and even violent means to force their views on others, they set about changing the hearts and minds of men.

"But the radicals up North couldn't be bothered with all that. They couldn't be bothered with persuading people and building support over time. They couldn't debate the issue and then accept the results of fair and democratic votes. Oh no. They could only condemn everyone who disagreed with them, calling us 'hate-filled' even as they employed the most hateful rhetoric against us. Instead of a reasonable and rational debate of the issues, they could only make personal attacks, accusing us of having evil motives that few of us, if any, actually have. They spread propaganda suggesting that every slave owner is a sadistic monster constantly applying the bullwhip, as if most farmers aren't smart enough to take good care of their livestock. And when they had worked themselves into enough of a frenzy, they began breaking the law and violating our constitutional rights.

"Article Four of the Constitution specifically requires the return of fugitive slaves, but for years the abolitionists have actively encouraged slaves to escape and refused to return them. They're so proud of their precious 'Underground Railroad,' but it is, in fact, a direct violation of our specifically delineated constitutional rights, not to mention theft of property. Men get strung up for stealing horses; why should those who steal slaves get any less?"

Several of the men nodded in agreement.

"As these illegal activities increased, Congress responded with a new Fugitive Slave Act designed to uphold Article Four. What was the response from the Northern states? Why, all of a sudden they were in favor of states' rights, declaring that they had the right to nullify federal laws. The Vermont legislature immediately passed a law that not only sought to nullify the Fugitive Slave Act, but that required state and local law enforcement officials to *assist* runaway slaves! The Wisconsin Supreme Court not only declared the Fugitive Slave Act unconstitutional, it even tried to overturn a U. S. Supreme Court decision upholding it. The *New-York Tribune* applauded Wisconsin and encouraged other Northern states to pursue 'the goal of state independence.' Salmon P. Chase, now Lincoln's Secretary of the Treasury, declared on the Senate floor that Congress did not have to abide by the rulings of the U. S. Supreme Court. Yet we're the rebels? What hypocrites!

"William Lloyd Garrison, the greatest rabble-rouser of them all, publicly burned a copy of the U. S. Constitution, calling it 'a Covenant with death and an agreement with Hell.' Now, if Northerners want to nullify the Constitution and burn every copy of it, I won't try to stop them. But how in heaven's name can they turn around and demand that we remain under the very Constitution they have just rejected; the very Constitution they've been violating; the very Constitution they've tried to nullify?"

McFall's voice was rising again, his gestures becoming more dramatic. He stretched out one arm and tapped the air with his finger.

"Mark that down: It was the Northern states that passed nullification laws. It was the Northern states that rebelled against the U. S. Constitution, violating specific clauses therein. It was the Northern states that said individual states don't have to listen to the federal government. In doing so, they invalidated the contract that created this union. And when one party violates the provisions of a contract, the other party or parties are automatically freed from that contract. James Madison himself, the primary author of the Constitution, said, 'a breach of any one article by any one party, leaves all other parties at liberty to consider the whole convention as dissolved.'

"If anyone will take the time to read the Ordinances of Secession and the Declarations of Causes passed by the Confederate states, they'll see that this was the reason the South severed the union. Not only were we *not* claiming the right to nullify federal law, we were complaining about those who did! Every single Confederate proclamation states plainly that the right to secede results directly from the invalidation of the Constitution by the North's long-term violation of its provisions. Period. The only 'states' right' we're claiming is the right to leave the union after other states invalidated the contract that binds us together.

"It's true that the South seceded in order to preserve the institution of slavery, but what gave us the right to secede was the fact that the institution of slavery was guaranteed to us under the

Constitution. Had it not been specifically guaranteed to us, or had they taken the time to change the rules through fair and democratic means, we would not have left. Isn't that right?"

He looked around the table. Several men nodded their heads.

"And there is something else guaranteed to us by the Constitution that they have ignored. I am a God-fearing Christian, but the Constitution of the United States promises us freedom of religion. In America, no one is supposed to be able to impose their religious beliefs on others. Yet the Yankee abolitionists, professing Christians to a man, have trampled on this principle, trying and succeeding in injecting their personal religious beliefs into politics. They preach against slavery from their church pulpits, openly endorsing abolitionist candidates, a clear violation of the separation of church and state. They've practiced violence in the name of religion in Virginia, Kansas, and elsewhere. And they finally succeeded in electing an abolitionist government, one willing to kill hundreds of thousands of its own citizens in order to impose a narrow set of moral values on everyone, completely outside the democratic process.

"No less than William H. Seward, now Lincoln's esteemed Secretary of State, stood on the floor of Congress and announced that 'there is a higher law than the Constitution.' Obviously he means God, and obviously he believes that he speaks for God, judges for God, and has the right to kill for God. Our Founding Fathers sought to establish a democratic republic, but the abolitionists, in a single election, have turned America into a tyrannical theocracy."

McFall was speaking loudly now, and for the first time he appeared to let his emotions guide his words. Even so, Tommy sensed that, underneath it all, his boss was fully in control of what he was saying.

"Whatever happened to freedom of choice?" he implored, holding his hands out in front of him and curling his fingers as if grasping for the elusive liberty of which he spoke. "If you don't want to own a slave, don't own one. That's your choice. But don't try to force your moral values on me. When it comes to slavery in the territories, all we've ever asked is to let the people of each new state choose. Popular sovereignty—let the people decide. The South is pro-choice. It's the anti-slavery forces who seek to take away our freedom of choice and tell us what to do with our own property."

McFall stopped abruptly and looked around, as if coming out of a trance. He sat down again.

"I'm sorry; I've strayed from my topic. But I think a true picture of our motives is important, because the Yankees have purposefully mischaracterized those motives. If they win the war, they will write those lies into the history books, teaching future generations that we were all traitors, and that we gave our lives for no other reason than to perpetuate evils upon slaves that most of us don't even own. Well, we know our true motives, and we know that our motives are pure and perhaps noble, even if we grant that slavery itself is wrong.

"We would not—I would not—consider the actions I'm proposing if I thought we had any alternative. What we are about to do, we are forced to do, and it is Lincoln himself who is forcing us. After all, the last thing we need right now is to divert resources away from fighting the enemy. But now that he is arming our slaves, he has made them our enemy. He has left us no choice. If anyone disagrees, let him speak now, and I'll call the whole thing off."

McFall knew by now that his audience was under his control. He waited, and again there was only silence. His voice shifted to a softer tone.

"I know every man here feels as badly about this as I do. It might help some of you to know that science is on our side."

The men all looked at him curiously as he reached down and pulled a book and some papers out of his satchel. He placed the book on the table and used one hand to slide it down to the middle.

"This is a book by a British scientist named Charles Darwin. It's called *On the Origin of Species*. It was published five years ago in England and four years ago in America. You may have heard of Darwin's theory that species compete for survival through something called 'natural selection,' and that through this process, animals develop from lower to higher orders. Applying this to humans, Darwinism teaches us that the different races have developed at different rates and in different ways, leaving some more advanced than others. It teaches us that some races are better suited to leadership, science, and the arts, while others are better suited to toil. We already knew that, but now we have scientific proof. Darwinism justifies slavery.

"Not only does it justify slavery, it also justifies the extermination of weaker species." He lifted the papers in his hand and referred to them. "Darwin specifically said, and I quote, 'the varieties of man seem to act on each other in the same way as different species of animals—the stronger always extirpating the weaker.' This was after European settlers had almost wiped out the Aborigines in Van Diemen's Land—or Tasmania, as it was recently renamed. The few that were left were removed, similar to the way our Indians were removed to the West. Darwin, while touring Australia, called these actions 'cruel' but 'unavoidable,' and expressed satisfaction that, again I quote, 'Van Diemen's Land enjoys the great advantage of being free from a native population.' Darwin himself supported the subjugation and even elimination of weaker races by those stronger and more advanced, because that is natural selection at work.

"We here in the South were Darwinists before Darwin. We've always known that the Negroid race was inferior to the Caucasian. Now science confirms that we were right.

"Darwinism says that we developed into humans over time, and clearly the Negro lags behind. You wouldn't call a newly laid egg a chicken, or a tadpole a frog. Until a person has developed to a certain point, they are not fully human, and they therefore have no rights, not even the right to life. Such is the case with the Negro.

"Just last year, we lost a distinguished gentleman from South Carolina named William J. Grayson, a former congressman and a published poet. You're familiar with his 1855 poem entitled 'The Hireling and the Slave.' In that poem, Mr. Grayson coined the term 'master race' to refer to Caucasians in relation to the lesser-developed races such as the Negro. I wonder if he knew before his death that science had confirmed the appropriateness of his phraseology.

"And just one year after Grayson's poem, a book by a French-man named de Gobineau was translated into English. It's called *The Moral and Intellectual Diversity of Races*. De Gobineau had also come to the conclusion that Caucasians are the superior race, and he suggested that the purest Caucasians are those from Northern Europe and Scandinavia. He called these the 'Aryan' race, and I don't have to point out to you that they are the forebears of most white Southerners. While the North has allowed itself to be contaminated through mixing with inferior stock from all over the world, we in the South have remained closest to the Aryan ideal.

"Yes, gentlemen, we are the master race, and science confirms it. Unfortunately, the abolitionists, like all religious fanatics, want to jettison the scientific method in favor of their personal religious beliefs. Clinging to their Bibles, they want to ignore the plain scientific evidence before them and pretend that all races are exactly alike, when science clearly says they are not. In doing so, they seek to upset the natural order. They seek to give freedom to millions of people who are not ready for it. Those chosen by nature to lead will not be allowed to lead, while those chosen by nature to toil will have their jobs taken from them. The con-sequences will be disastrous for both black and white, for both North and South.

"The program I am suggesting may sound terrible at first, but we can see that it's really just part of Darwin's process of natural selection. If we lose this war and the slaves are freed, there will be a Darwinian struggle between the two races here in the South. Such a struggle is unavoidable, because there's only so much land and so much food to go around. But the struggle won't be a fair one, because the blacks will be backed by the Yankees' guns.

"Lincoln himself says he doesn't think blacks and whites can co-exist peacefully. By eliminating the Negro now, we will main-tain the natural order, protect ourselves from the revenge of our former slaves, and avoid a race war. It is, in my opinion, the only way to avoid a race war."

He paused. All the men were staring into space thoughtfully. Once again, McFall gave them a few moments to think, which made his next statement all the more dramatic.

"I fully expect to be executed for what I'm about to do," he said.

Tommy looked up at him in surprise.

"I would not undertake such an unpleasant task were I not convinced of its necessity. If I thought there was another solution to this problem, I would be the first to embrace it. But I think our choices are clear. We either sit idly by while our slaves are armed against us—which will guarantee that we lose the war—or we take action. I, for one, intend to take action."

Again he paused to allow the men to think about what he had said.

"Well, gentlemen, that concludes my presentation. For your protection, I won't go into detail regarding implementation, but I would be happy to share my plans with you upon request. Also for your protection, I'm going to assume that I'll have your department's cooperation. If you don't feel comfortable giving me that cooperation, simply drop by later today and tell me so. Either way, you'll be able to say in all honesty that you never agreed to anything."

Very clever, Tommy thought.

"Whether you fulfill my request or not, let me remind you that you are sworn never to discuss this with anyone outside this room. The civil and military leadership of the Confederacy know nothing of this, nor can they. We are the only people who know about it. Any questions should be directed to me personally. I will take full responsibility."

Just then, they heard the sound of doors opening and footsteps in the hallway above them.

"Perfect timing, gentlemen," McFall said with a smile. "If you have any questions or comments, I'll be in my office. Otherwise, have a good day."

As the men filed out, McFall remained seated, so Tommy did too. McFall pulled out his pocket watch and Tommy got a glimpse of the time. McFall had spoken for just over thirty minutes. In that brief time, the fate of millions had been sealed.

As soon as the last man left, McFall turned to his young aide. "What I said goes for you, too. You don't have to participate if you don't want to. Before you decide, let me tell you exactly what we'll be doing. We will only be coordinating this effort. You will never order anyone killed, nor will you ever be present when someone is killed. Your job will be purely administrative, just as it is now. In fact, you understand that we'll be coordinating this effort in addition to our usual duties, right?"

"Yes, sir, I understand," Tommy said.

"And if it helps any, let me point out that this program will move forward with you or without you. Your participation will not result in a single death that would not have happened anyway, nor will your lack of participation save anyone. I could use your help, but if you're not comfortable with it, you have the same right to withdraw as anyone else."

Tommy said, "Thank you, sir," but then he said nothing else. McFall, seeing that he was thinking, waited for a moment.

"Did you have any questions?"

Tommy hesitated, shifting slightly in his seat. McFall was quick to reassure him.

"You can ask me anything, you know. I said you don't have to participate if you don't want to, so it can't possibly hurt to ask questions."

"Well," Tommy said shyly, "when you said we have to eliminate the Negro, did you mean the women and children too?"

McFall nodded solemnly. "Yes, I'm afraid I did."

"But why? It's the males who are being armed against us."

McFall nodded again, the look on his face signifying that he understood the seriousness of the question.

"Well, you remember I talked about the slave revolt in Haiti?" Tommy nodded. "When the French troops evacuated, they left behind nearly a thousand men who were bedridden with malaria and yellow fever. The new revolutionary president, Jean-Jacques Dessalines, had them drowned. Not shot, but drowned. The remaining white civilians tried to flee the island, but Dessalines put out orders to stop them. He then went from city to city, personally assuring that the whites were slaughtered—men, women, and children. Around five thousand in all. His explanation to his people was simple: We can't be free of this problem if we leave alive the next generation and the women who can breed the generation after that. The same is true in our situation.

"But that's just part of the reason. You see, after Dessalines massacred all the whites on the island, he made a huge mistake. He didn't try to keep his massacre a secret—he even tried to justify it to the world. The result was exactly what you would expect—diplomatic and trade relations were severed by almost every civilized nation, leaving Haiti isolated, ushering in an extended period of poverty and instability. We don't want the same thing to happen here.

"We have to think about what will happen to the South after this conflict finally ends. If we prevail, outside knowledge of this program would make it difficult for our new nation to establish relationships with other nations. If we lose, the North will use our actions against us, even though they're the ones who forced us into it. It's essential that this program be carried out in utmost secrecy, and maintaining that secrecy requires the elimination of *all* the slaves, not just the men.

"Think about it. If an entire family of slaves disappears in the middle of a war, few people will notice. Everyone will assume they fled north. But if we leave a couple million Negro widows and orphans wandering the back roads of the South, what we have done will be obvious to everyone. And again, where would those people live, and how would they eat? That's why this program has to include them. There is no partial solution to this problem. It has to be a final solution, or it won't be a solution at all. Does that make sense?"

Tommy nodded, still deep in thought. McFall stood up and patted him on the shoulder.

"Look, why don't you think about it overnight? Put it to prayer. We can talk about it in the morning."

"Thank you, sir."

But Tommy didn't wait until nightfall to think about it—he couldn't get it out of his mind the whole day. Not a single officer from the morning's meeting came by, so he knew the program was going to go forward with or without him. As the workday was ending, he decided he might as well get it off his chest. He stepped inside his boss's office and closed the door to keep from being overheard.

"I just wanted to let you know I'm on board, sir."

"Oh, okay," McFall said nonchalantly. "You don't want to think about it overnight?"

"There's no need. I don't like it, but I don't think the Yankees have given us any choice. We can't just sit idly by while they arm our own slaves against us. No military on Earth would allow that to happen."

McFall nodded, smiling slightly at hearing his own words parroted back to him.

"Very well. Tomorrow morning we start implementation. And may God have mercy on our souls."

Four

THE PROGRAM

OMMY PUT HIS ARM UP to protect his face from the intense heat of the blast furnaces at the Tredegar Iron Works in Richmond. He staggered back a step and wondered how anyone could work so close to these roaring behemoths. It took two brawny men to swing the huge iron door closed on the searing heat. When it clamped shut, the temperature dropped so suddenly that the humid May air, which felt hot to him on the way over, now chilled his sweating face.

"It won't work!" shouted the foreman over the roar of the furnaces. "It takes too much fuel!"

Colonel McFall nodded, his lips pursed. The five Negro cadavers they had placed in the furnace were not as easily incinerated as had been hoped. The fuel required to dispose of large numbers of bodies, and the manpower it would take to collect it, could simply not be spared at this point in the war. This was a setback. But they were already working on other methods.

The first priority of the program was to eliminate slaves in imminent danger of being freed by the Yankees. Doing so would require companies of men operating close to the front lines. It would be a dangerous assignment, made more dangerous by the inevitable resistance from the slave owners themselves. The entire philosophical foundation of the Confederacy was that slaves were the property of their masters and the government had no right to take away that property. Yet now, out of necessity, they were going to have to violate their own sacred principle. They were sure to be met with resistance, and if word got out, they might even meet organized resistance. The teetering Confederacy could not afford such an internal conflict. Protocols for dealing with slave owners had to be worked out and tested carefully.

Even forming these front-line execution squads presented a logistical challenge. Men who might be open to such an assignment had to be recruited one by one, and in secret, to avoid having word spread through the military that the South was going to start killing slaves. There was already a problem with soldiers deserting their posts to protect their homes and families against the Yankees—if they thought they had to protect their property against their own side, the army might disintegrate.

By the early summer, five squads of fifteen to twenty men had been formed, one in the Trans-Mississippi Theater and four spread across the Western and Eastern Theaters, from northern Mississippi to central Virginia. Once formed, these squads operated with autonomy and flexibility, staying one step ahead of Northern advances. Meanwhile, Colonel McFall and his young aide worked on a more comprehensive approach. The blast furnace test was a disappointing first effort in that direction.

Disposal of the bodies, essential to hiding the nature of the program, was their biggest obstacle. When visiting isolated farms, the execution squads could force the slaves to dig their own graves before shooting them. But this wouldn't work even in small towns, much less in the bigger cities that had larger Negro populations. A different approach would be necessary if they were to accelerate the process.

A plan was developed for a network of "processing camps" in isolated spots close to rail lines. Orders would be given to send all runaway and abandoned slaves to these camps for "detention." In reality, the slaves would be forced to dig mass graves, then lined up and shot. Once the system was in place, measures would be taken to increase the number of slaves brought to the camps.

In early June, Tommy and his boss left Richmond to supervise the establishment of the first camp on the border of Georgia and Alabama. The spot chosen was suitably isolated. When they arrived, work crews had already laid a spur from the rail line off into open country. The spur ran about a mile from the main track, then simply stopped. Over the next week, crews rode in on a special work train and cordoned off an area of four square acres with wire fences. Inside, they built simple wooden huts—a tiny office, a kitchen, a supply building, and two barracks, one for the soldiers and one for the slaves. The supply building was stocked with rifles and shovels. The slave barracks was surrounded by a second fence.

Colonel McFall and Tommy stood evaluating the finished camp. It was clean, neat, and sparse. A four-car train could pull right into the encampment and the gate close behind it. The land at the far end sloped gently away at an angle, so the burial pits would be just out of sight. The slave barracks was only for those kept alive for burial duty—most would be executed upon arrival.

The camp guards, who would double as firing squads, were handpicked. To run the camp, Colonel McFall selected a rough sergeant named Smithson and elevated him to the rank of captain.

Tommy thought Smithson to be the nastiest man he'd ever met, from his hygiene to his language. But perhaps that was the type of man needed to run such a camp.

While all this was going on, they received word that Grant's army had descended on Richmond and laid siege to nearby Petersburg. McFall was ordered to set up headquarters in Montgomery and handle his duties from there. He and Tommy continued to administer the elimination program as best they could, but their attention was increasingly drawn to more immediate military concerns. On September 2nd, Sherman captured Atlanta. The Yankees now occupied land between Montgomery and the Confederate capitol, making it too dangerous to return.

"We should have started earlier," McFall said to Tommy. "It's not going to be enough." McFall had seen the need for the program of elimination before anyone else, and now he saw that they were not going to achieve their goal. In fact, he had seen before anyone else that the South was going to lose the war. Tommy couldn't help wondering what would have happened had his boss been given a higher level of leadership earlier in the war. Perhaps a man of his vision could have made a difference in the course of the war and avoided the necessity of this messy program.

By the end of 1864, the Confederacy was just trying to hold on. Telegraph lines and railroads throughout the South were regularly disrupted, and railcars were at a premium. There wasn't enough food to feed the army, much less thousands of slaves during shipping and processing. As a result, the number of slaves coming to the processing camp never amounted to more than a trickle, and a second processing camp was never established. In the end, the bulk of the task fell to the execution squads.

Five

THE EXECUTION SQUADS

HIRAM BLEDSOE AND HIS FAMILY were relieved to see the company of Confederate soldiers riding up their lane. He motioned to his young son to take the reins of the officers' horses as they dismounted.

"I'm Captain Matthews," the first officer said, shaking the farmer's hand. "This is Lieutenant Watkins."

"We heard the shooting last night," Hiram said. "Sure glad you were able to drive them off."

"Yes," said Captain Matthews, "but they'll be back. And soon. Could I get water for my horses and men?"

"Around back," Hiram said. He nodded to his son, who led the captain's horse around the side of the house. The other soldiers followed.

"May I have a word with you in private?"

"Certainly," Hiram said. As the two men strolled together away from the house, his wife and daughters turned to go back inside.

"I'm afraid I have to inform you that we're consolidating our forces to the rear," Matthews said. "That means the Yankees could get here as early as tomorrow."

Hiram Bledsoe nodded, a grim look on his face.

"Obviously we knew they were getting closer. What do you think they'll do to us?"

"Well, the first thing they'll do is free your slaves. And as you probably know, there are stories of the Yankees looking the other way while slaves take revenge on their former masters." He paused for effect. "And on their former masters' wives and daughters." From the corner of his eye he saw the man grimace. "After that, they'll give your slaves guns and put them in battle to kill Confederate soldiers. Do you have any sons in the army?"

"Yes, my oldest."

"So, your son could be killed in battle by someone's slave. And your slaves could end up killing someone else's son."

"So what should we do?"

"My men and I are on special assignment to make sure these things don't happen. Our orders are to take your slaves to the rear lines to keep them out of Yankee hands. We can leave you one or two female slaves over the age of fifty."

"Will we get them back after this is over?"

"I'm afraid I can't make any guarantees at this point. But if we don't take them, the Yankees will."

Hiram nodded again. "Yes, I understand. Do you think we should leave?"

"That's a choice each person has to make. If it were me, I probably would. Do you have some place to go?"

"My brother's down in Amory. But what about the house? What about the farm?"

Matthews shook his head sympathetically. "That's the question. They may torch it if you're not here. Then again, they may torch it if you are here. Either way, they'll take every bit of food you have, butcher every animal to feed their troops. At least in Amory you and your family will be safe and fed." Matthews stopped walking and looked out over the fields. "Quite a predicament your fellow 'countrymen' have put you in, isn't it?"

Hiram snorted derisively and spit on the ground. "They're not my countrymen, and they never will be again. Win or lose."

"Yep. Well, we need to keep moving. I'll need your slaves to be ready in fifteen minutes. No more than one small bag each. My clerk will record their names as your property while we walk. And if I were you, I'd have the family ready to go first thing in the morning."

An hour or so later, Hiram stood on his veranda, looking out over his farm for what he knew might be the last time. His family and his oldest house slave were inside packing. The rest of his slaves had gone with the Confederate soldiers. His ears perked up at a rifle report from off in the distance, followed a few minutes later by a second. He waited to hear if the shots continued, but heard nothing more.

It was only later, as he lay in bed unable to sleep, that he realized the rifle reports had come from the direction the soldiers had taken. Had the Yankees worked their way around to that side? If so, he and his family might not be able to get through the next day. But there had been only two volleys, not the crackling sound they had heard the day before when the two sides exchanged fire. As he played the sound over in his mind, he was sure it had been the sound of multiple rifles firing in unison.

He had almost dozed off when the truth hit him. He sat up in bed, his eyes wide. After a few minutes, he convinced himself he was just imagining things. Still, it was a restless night.

Early the next morning, he steered the wagon team out of their lane and onto the dusty road the soldiers had taken the night before. His wife, knowing he hadn't slept well, spoke only when necessary. She didn't realize that his silence wasn't because of lack of sleep. He was looking for something.

Sure enough, when they had gone about the right distance, he spotted a fresh mound of dirt off the road and partially hidden by trees. He didn't say anything to his family, but his fingers gripped the reins in anger. Why did they have to kill them? Now who will bring in the crops? But the captain's words from the night before came back to him: The Yankees would have freed their slaves anyway. Still, why had the officer lied to him? But again the answer came to him right away: How would he have reacted had he been told the truth? The soldiers had done what they had to do.

· ·

When the execution squads first got started, they immediately ran into resistance from slave owners. The original plan had been to kill the slaves and bury them right there on the farms, but in order to do so, they had to sequester the owner and his family in their own home at gunpoint while the graves were being dug. This meant leaving behind an angry family, and every family was armed.

It was Colonel McFall who suggested the story about taking the slaves to the rear lines for "protection." When this approach worked, it relieved the tension and greatly improved the speed and efficiency of the execution squads. This story was also used to explain why slaves were being loaded onto railcars.

Sometimes opportunities presented themselves. The execution squads came upon more than one farm where the owners had already fled, leaving their slaves behind. Or they found slaves working in the field, watched over by one or two overseers. It was a simple matter to disarm the overseers and shoot the slaves. Harvest time was easiest, because they could simply leave the slaves where they fell, hidden by the crops. By this point in the war, Yankee scouts were so used to the sight of buzzards, they didn't think to ask why the birds were circling ahead of the fighting instead of behind it.

Occasionally, the execution squads created their own opportunities.

· ·

Captain Jim Young was unhappy. He'd come South to fight the Rebels, but he didn't get along with his commanding officer, so once again he found himself leading a ragged band of liberated slaves back to the rear lines. He kept his horse walking faster than the slaves could follow, partly out of impatience and partly out of disdain for the "darkies" who were keeping him from battle. With their children in tow and their belongings carried in bundles or loaded on makeshift carts, the freedmen struggled to keep up.

Just as they reached a dusty crossroads, a Union messenger came galloping up, his horse wet with sweat.

"Sir! Major Honeycutt is engaged at Swan's Bluff and needs reinforcements fast!" The messenger pointed down one of the crossroads, indicating the route to the action.

Captain Young couldn't have been happier at the interruption. He turned in his saddle and waved his hand.

"Forward, men! Double time!" The soldiers left the slaves and followed him onto the crossroad. They began a steady jog to the rhythm of their sergeant's barking cadence, the officers on their horses trotting ahead.

"What about the slaves?" his lieutenant asked.

"What about them?" the captain retorted. "We're here to fight a war, not babysit niggers."

The slaves stood watching the soldiers disappear in a cloud of dust. They turned to look at the messenger. He jerked his head in the direction he had come from and said, "Come on." Turning, he led them down the road. Unlike the captain, he kept his horse at a comfortable pace for the caravan behind him, but now it was the slaves who hurried along. They may have been liberated according to the official position of the United States government, but they were runaway slaves in Confederate eyes, and now they had no protection except a single soldier armed with pistols.

They had gone no more than half a mile when the messenger threw his hand up, then wheeled around and put his finger to his lips to signal them to be quiet. The slaves stopped in their tracks. "Did you hear something?" he whispered loudly. The slaves looked all around, seeing nothing but trees on both sides of the road. Instinctively they clung to each other, their eyes darting nervously. They all jumped as one when they heard a loud snap from the woods to their side.

For a moment they were confused by a rustling sound that seemed to come from all around them. Then their worst fears were realized. Rising up from the ground and stepping out from behind trees on both sides of the road were Confederate soldiers. Even more confusing was the reaction of the Union messenger.

He had been watching the slaves in their discomfort, and now he leaned back in his saddle and roared with laughter. Some of the Confederate soldiers joined him.

"Nice work, Ben."

"Thanks. Did you see them jump?"

"Like a frog on a hot skillet," said one Confederate with a guffaw.

"The whites of their eyes would have glowed in the dark," said another.

"Hey, Ben, need some more 'sweat' for your horse?" The soldier held out his canteen and shook it, eliciting chuckles from those around him. Ben, pulling his gray uniform pants from his saddlebag, waved him off with a smile. The men grinned at the subterfuge they had just pulled off, but the rest of the soldiers weren't laughing as they surrounded the slaves.

"Let's move on up the road a bit," an officer yelled, waving his arm.

As the slaves moved forward, their shoulders sagged in despair. They knew they were about to be returned to slavery, and no doubt punished harshly. It was a horrible disappointment after being so close to freedom.

The procession went over a slight rise and around a curve, at which point the side of the road dropped off into a deep ravine on the left.

"Hold up!" shouted the officer, raising his hand. "You're moving too slow. We're going to have to get rid of the carts and stuff. I want everything thrown into the ravine. Now!"

Bayonets bristling around them, the slaves moved toward the side of the road. Soldiers knocked the bags from their hands and kicked them over the side. The other slaves followed suit, throwing their only earthly possessions over the edge.

"Now the carts. Hurry!"

One by one the carts were sent crashing down into the ravine.

"Now line up on that side of the road facing forward."

Several soldiers pushed and pulled the slaves into a single file line. The slaves thought they were going to be marched on up the road, but as soon as they were in place, the officer barked out another order.

"Turn to your right," he shouted. "That's this direction."

The slaves did as they were told, and when they did, they were shocked to see the soldiers lined up in the formation of a firing squad, their rifles already raised.

"Fire!" cried the officer.

The guns exploded and half the slaves fell to the ground, some of them toppling over backwards into the ravine. The women screamed and the children cried out. The women quickly realized that every adult male had been shot. They dropped to their knees to see if the men were still alive. In their anguish, none of them noticed that the soldiers were calmly reloading. As soon as the soldiers were ready, the officer addressed the remaining slaves.

"Okay, that's enough! Stand up! I said stand up!"

A few soldiers walked down the line, pulling the women up and pushing them into a straight line again. In the few seconds this took, the women realized they were next. Before they could react, the order was given, the rifles fired, and once again bodies fell. Pistols and bayonets took care of those remaining, most of them children. It was an easy matter to shove the bodies into the ravine. No one coming down the road from either direction would see the carnage below.

. . . .

Another successful strategy, again conceived by McFall, took advantage of the widespread use of local slaves for burial duty after battles and skirmishes. As soon as the shooting stopped, the execution squads presented themselves as special companies assigned to manage this unsavory task, a claim supported by the shovels strapped to their pack horses. The Confederate military officers, unaware of their true intent, were happy to leave the job with them. The slaveholders had no problem lending their slaves for the proper burial of soldiers who had died defending the South. No one had any way of knowing that the squads were rounding up far more slaves than were needed, many of whom never even made it to the battlefield. Once the Confederate dead had been buried and the squads started taking the remaining slaves back to their owners, it was a simple matter to detour into the woods and hand out the shovels again. By the time the owners realized their slaves weren't coming back, the execution squad was already well down the road.

Operating so close to the front lines, the squads sometimes had to act with haste. There were still times when they had to sequester families and kill the slaves on the spot. The only good thing about these situations was the extra time it gave the officers to explain things to the family while the graves were being dug. Although these were slave owners, they were, for the most part, peaceful farmers who had never seen anyone killed. Having someone murdered on their farm would have been shocking enough to these simple people, but to have their slaves mowed down with no forewarning was horrifying. The officers impressed upon them the equally horrifying alternative of having their slaves freed and armed against them, or allowed to exact their revenge. By the time the soldiers had spent enough time with a family, they usually joined in cursing Abraham Lincoln for forcing them into this hellish predicament.

There was not just anger, but sadness, as well. This would have surprised most Northerners, who had little direct contact with blacks, and who never realized how closely Southerners and their slaves co-existed. On the smaller farms, slave owners worked the fields side-by-side with their slaves. Female slaves helped raise the slave owners' children, just as their parents had helped raise the slave owners. The children of slaves played with the children of slave owners. The distinction between the two was never lost, but field slaves were often treated much like hired hands, and it wasn't uncommon for house slaves to be thought of as part of the family. It was an odd relationship, but one that had existed between master and slave at least since the days of ancient Rome.

. . . .

Captain Matthews and his men came to a plantation farm-house with a single row of slave shacks running perpendicular behind it. When they pulled up in front of the house, the wife came out, accompanied by a ten-year-old boy and two daughters, none of whom noticed that a couple of the soldiers went right on around the side of the house.

"Afternoon, ma'am," Matthews said, doffing his hat. "I'm Captain Matthews. This is Lieutenant Watkins. Is your husband home?"

"He's down at the end of the north field," she said, nodding past the soldiers and across the road. "The reaper broke down." Matthews and his men turned to look behind them. Four or five men were visible way off in the distance.

"Just a minute, I'll call 'em." Turning, she took hold of a rope hanging from a bell by the front door and rang it loudly seven or eight times. The men at the end of the field looked up, then back down at their work.

"They'll be along shortly," the woman said. "Can I get you some food or water?"

"Some water would be nice," Matthews said, dismounting.

"You can water the horses 'round back," she said.

Matthews looked at his lieutenant and nodded toward the back of the house. Speaking too low for the woman to hear, he said, "Let's get this done before the menfolk get here." Watkins nodded and waved for the rest of the soldiers to follow him.

Matthews and a few of his men followed the woman into the house. He went through the usual procedure, explaining the situation to the wife, then sequestering the family in a front room under guard. By the time he went out through the back door, Watkins and his men had the slaves out of their sheds and lined up. The soldiers were handing out shovels. Just then a lookout came around the side of the house to inform Matthews that the men in the field had started their way.

"We're going to have to hurry," Matthews said quietly to Watkins. "Shoot first, dig after."

Watkins nodded and started to turn to his men, then stopped and looked back at the house. Matthews also turned to look. The soldiers were bringing the house slaves out—a woman in her forties along with a girl of around twenty and a boy around six or seven. Matthews started to turn right back, but the extraordinary beauty of the young woman held his gaze. She had an exotic caramel coloring and fine features. The boy, whom the girl held close by her side, was mulatto. Matthews had assumed they were the children of the older woman, but the variance in their shading, and the way the girl held the boy, made him suspect he was actually looking at three generations.

The soldiers put them in line with the other slaves. They tied the slaves' hands behind their backs and placed blindfolds on them. The soldiers lined up, the order was given, the firing hammers struck, and the slaves fell. The whole time, Matthews couldn't take his eyes off the girl. He didn't know why, but taking the life of this beautiful young woman seemed even worse than killing the child by her side.

"Okay, stack 'em up," Watkins ordered.

Matthews turned back toward the house, and just as he did, the plantation owner and his three sons came around the side of the house. Soldiers were keeping them in check, and one soldier was wrestling a firearm away from the oldest son. The man's ten-year-old son burst out of the back door, having bolted around the guards when he saw his dad through the front window.

Matthews took a deep breath and started toward them, ready to repeat his usual explanation and steeling himself for the usual protests. But when he addressed the owner, the man paid no attention. He was looking at his fallen slaves with an intensity of despair that Matthews had not seen before. His face was convulsed into pure shock and sorrow, without any of the anger they were used to seeing. Matthews followed the man's gaze and saw that he was looking at one particular point. He nodded to the soldiers to let him pass.

The man ran directly to the beautiful young woman, dropping to his knees beside her, touching her face to confirm the awful truth. He looked at the boy and did the same, simultaneously reaching to his left to touch the shoulder of the older woman. Even from behind it was clear that he was sobbing. Then he took the young woman in his arms and lifted her lifeless body to his chest, holding her as his sobs became audible. He looked down and stroked her cheek, bathing her face in his tears. He reached over and grasped the boy's shirt, wadding it in his hand and pulling his body close up against that of his mother. Twice he swayed toward the older woman, wanting to include her in his grief, but having no more arms with which to hold her.

Everyone in the yard stood stock still, staring. There was no sound except for the man's sobbing, which seemed to echo off the low gray sky. The ten-year-old, distraught over his father's grief but too young to understand the obvious implications, also started crying. He lunged at the nearest soldier, pounding him with his small fists. The soldier let him strike several times before reaching down and hugging the sobbing boy against his body. Matthews looked at the other sons. Two of them stood with blank looks on their faces, but the third had a look of disgust. Perhaps this son had suspected the truth all along.

The man's sobs finally began to play out. Watkins stepped forward, put his hand on the man's shoulder, then reached under his arm to help him up. The man reluctantly stood up, still looking down at the three bodies. Watkins pulled his arm to turn him away from the sight, and now Matthews could see that his cheeks were wet with tears. Watkins motioned with his other hand for his men to remove the bodies along with the rest.

Matthews turned toward the sons to talk to them, but when he did, he saw the grieving man's wife standing on the back porch. He didn't know how long she had been standing there, but it had obviously been long enough. Her hands were clenched into fists planted firmly on her hips. Her face, which had been so pleasant when they had arrived, was pulled taut with anger. Her eyes were narrow slits.

When the sons saw Matthews looking at the house, they turned and saw her, too. When they turned back to look at their dad, Matthews also turned to look back at him. The man had seen his wife standing there, and his face had gone as white as a sheet. He had been so lost in his grief that he had been completely unaware of his surroundings or his actions. Now he knew he had given away his great secret. He visibly sagged, forcing Watkins to shift his weight to hold him up by his arm. For a long moment, no one said anything.

"Billy, hitch the wagon," the woman said through gritted teeth, her eyes still on her husband.

"Gladly," said the son with the disgusted look on his face. Looking straight at his father, he threw the tools he was carrying to the ground and started toward the stables.

"Lee, get inside and get cleaned up," the woman said. "Now." The ten-year-old boy reluctantly obeyed. The wife gave one last look at the crestfallen husband before following the boy inside.

Matthews turned back to look at the husband. He had been in enough battles to recognize a man in shock. And who could expect anything else in a man who had just lost two families in an instant?

Watkins eased the sagging man to the ground, then signaled his men to grab the shovels and get to work. The man sat on the ground, his eyes focused on nothing. Matthews turned to the remaining two sons and tried to pick up where he had left off. He surmised from their reactions that they would be no trouble. He lifted his arm to point to the spot where he thought they should dig, but as he turned, he saw the farm owner pull something from his boot. Before he could say a word, the man's hand went up to his head, there was a pop, and he fell over dead.

For the second time, everyone froze. Matthews's arm hung in the air, still pointing. He looked back at the two sons to see what their reaction would be, but by now they shared their brother's disgust.

"Go tell Mom there's no need to leave," said one. "I'll tell Billy."

Matthews had to follow the young man to finish asking his question.

"Uh, I thought we'd dig the pit down at the end of the shacks."

"That's fine," the young man said without breaking his stride.

"And what about your father? Do you have a family plot?"

"Bury him with the slaves," came the reply.

Later, as the soldiers moved on down the road, no one spoke. After a while, Watkins brought his horse over close to Matthews and cleared his throat.

"Okay, just so I'm clear on this . . ."

"Yes?"

"I mean, do you read it the same way I do? The mother and the daughter both . . ."

"Yes, I read it that way."

"So his own daughter . . ."

"Yep."

"But she couldn't have been more than twenty or twenty-one, and her son was at least six or seven."

"Yep."

Watkins was silent for a moment.

"So that bastard got what he deserved."

"Yep."

Six

DISARRAY

"YOU WERE RIGHT," TOMMY SAID, dropping a military communiqué onto McFall's desk one cold January day in 1865. "They're taking our land and giving it to the slaves."

Union general William Tecumseh Sherman, having completed his infamous "March to the Sea," had issued Special Field Order #15, giving forty acres of land to every freed slave in the area. Sherman's orders specifically allocated "the islands from Charleston, south, the abandoned rice fields along the rivers for thirty miles back from the sea, and the country bordering the St. Johns River, Florida." His order appointed military officers to oversee the settlement of the slaves on land previously owned by their masters. Colonel McFall's prediction had come true.

"Not the kind of thing you want to be right about," McFall said, "but there it is. And you'll notice it's the military giving away people's land. No due process, no legality at all. A military dictatorship, just as we feared. They're going to confiscate the South as spoils of war. That's been their plan all along."

Just two weeks later, on January 31, 1865, Congress passed the 13th amendment to the U. S. Constitution, abolishing slavery. Ratification by the Northern states was sure to be swift. To

Southerners, this confirmed that the goal of the war had always been to end slavery, despite Lincoln's repeated assurances that it was only about keeping the union intact. And if the slaves had really been the cause of all this bloodshed and destruction, how were Southerners supposed to feel about them?

These two actions, coming on top of each other, provided clear justification for McFall's policy of elimination. A program that would have sounded horrible at the war's beginning, and that was controversial when he had presented it less than a year before, now sounded like solid military strategy and the obvious response to the actions of the Yankees. Besides, Sherman had just waged war against civilians from Atlanta to Savannah, burning homes and crops in a swath three hundred miles long and sixty miles wide, while the Yankee naval blockade kept food and medicine from people who desperately needed it. The scorched-earth tactics of the North made the program of elimination less horrible by comparison, and in any case, they made many in the South too angry to care.

McFall could now openly discuss the necessity of killing slaves, and for the first time he could even risk putting messages in writing. From his office in Montgomery, he began a campaign by telegraph and courier, urging military officers to shoot slaves when retreating to prevent them from being armed against the South. He encouraged others to spread the idea by word of mouth, but warned them to keep it away from the top civilian and military leaders. This was supposedly so the leaders wouldn't be culpable, but it was really to prevent them from shutting the program down.

Over the following weeks, reports filtered back that McFall's tactics were being implemented in various places. The further the Yankees penetrated into Confederate territory, the more things were in disarray, and the more unclaimed slaves there were to round up and send to the processing camp, or to shoot on the spot. The execution squads were ordered to double their efforts, using hit-and-run tactics whenever possible. They could no longer concern themselves with the slaveholders' feelings. Time was running out for the Confederacy.

Seven

"DEATH RIDERS"

CHICKENS SCATTERED AS PHIL DRINNON galloped his horse up to the white frame farmhouse. He swung out of his saddle so fast that his boots hit the ground simultaneously. He bounded up the steps onto the porch and banged on the door.

"Grady! Grady Morrison! Open up!"

"Who in heaven's name is that?" Grady asked his wife from his seat by the fire.

"It's Phil Drinnon," she said, peeping out the window. "And he's powerful upset about something."

Phil knocked again. "Grady! I need to talk to you!"

"Come on in," Grady called, rising from his seat. Phil opened the door and entered.

"They killed my slaves! Mowed 'em down out in the cow pasture!"

"What? Who?"

"Confederate soldiers, that's who. They were feeding the live-stock and this patrol rode by. They circled back and shot 'em all in cold blood. Dexter's barely hanging on; the other three are dead."

"Oh, my!" said Mrs. Morrison.

"I'm so sorry," Grady said. "You saw this happen?"

"No, Dexter's pickaninnies told us. They had followed the men down and were playing in the woods when it happened. If they hadn't been there to come fetch us, Dexter'd be dead too."

"But why would they do such a thing?" Mrs. Morrison asked, motioning for him to have a seat.

"That's what I wanted to know," he said, accepting her offer, but sitting on the edge of the chair and leaning forward as he talked. "So I asked Dexter to tell me about it. I wanted to report these guys to the nearest Confederate officer and, you know, file a claim for my damages."

Realizing how crass that sounded, Phil dipped his head in embarrassment. But Grady just nodded.

"Of course," he said in an understanding voice. "Go on."

"But he's still half delirious, and all I could get him to do was whisper one thing."

"What was that?"

"'Death riders.'"

"Death riders?" Mrs. Morrison repeated.

"That's all he would say. And when his wife Lucy came in and heard him say it, she made a quick shushing sound at him. So I let him rest and called her and the other women and old Joe into a room and closed the door. I made 'em tell me what they had heard. It took a long time to get 'em to talk. I could tell they were afraid. But I told the wives that if they knew something, it might help us stop these guys, maybe even avenge their husbands. Even then I had to act mighty angry to scare 'em into talking."

"So what did they say?" Mrs. Morrison asked, her eyes wide.

"It's just rumors, but they said there's been talk of squads of Rebel soldiers going around killing slaves to keep 'em from being freed by the Yankees and armed against the South." Mrs. Morrison seemed shocked, but Grady barely changed expression. "And there's more," Phil said.

"What?" Mrs. Morrison asked breathlessly.

"There are also rumors of death camps, where they take railcars full of slaves and line 'em up to be shot, then dumped into mass graves. Supposedly there's one south of here, down along the Georgia line somewhere. Don't know how many others. If it's true, it means they're trying to exterminate the Negro race."

"How horrible," Mrs. Morrison said, her hands to her face. She shook her head and made a "tch, tch" sound. Grady, however, had the traces of a bemused smile on this face. Phil looked at him with narrowed eyes.

"Okay, let's have it," he said, motioning with his hands.

Grady shrugged. "Well, come on. Are you really surprised by this?"

"Yes, I'm surprised, because it goes against everything the Confederacy stands for. The whole point of this war was to defend my constitutional right to own slaves. Now our own troops have taken them from me. And to kill them like that—what did they ever do to deserve that?" Mrs. Morrison shook her head, but Grady's look of benign condemnation didn't change. "I mean, we left the union because the North threatened to violate our rights. Now the Confederacy has actually done it."

"So what are you going to do," Grady asked, "secede from the seceders? Where would it end?" A tone of sarcasm had slipped into his speech.

Phil's eyes narrowed again. "Look, I'm fully aware of how amusing this is to you. I know where your sympathies lie. You think the South is reaping its just reward, and maybe you're right. That's why I came to you. I need your help."

"My help? What could I possibly do to help?"

"I need information, and you can get it."

"What kind of information?"

"Where this death camp is located, to begin with."

"And what makes you think I can get it?"

"This is no time to play games. We all know you're an abolitionist, and I know you're connected to the underground."

"I don't know what you're talking about."

"Sure you don't. Look, I disagree with your views on slavery, but on this matter we're together. Surely you want to see these men brought to justice, this killing stopped. Don't you?"

Grady looked at him for a long moment before answering.

"Suppose I can find out. What will you do about it?"

"I'm not sure. I guess take the information to the Union troops, to begin with."

"You'd have to go to Chattanooga to do that. Mighty cold ride this time of year, and you'd have to cross enemy lines."

"You get me the information, and I'll make the trip."

Again Grady paused before responding. Then he nodded.

"Okay, but you know this will take some time. Information travels faster when people are moving around. It's going to take longer this time of year."

More than two weeks passed before Phil received word that Grady wanted to see him.

"How's Dexter?" Grady asked.

"Much better, thanks. The doctor says he'll make a full recovery."

"Glad to hear it. Well, we got the information you wanted."

"Great! What'd they find out?"

"They found the death camp, and a couple of men rode out through the woods and eyeballed it from a distance. They said it's a pretty dinky affair, just a wire fence around some shacks, but there are three open pits full of bodies. The men who saw it said they were horrified that anything like that existed on Earth."

Phil shook his head in sympathy. "So how many guards?"

"That's the surprising thing. There was only one sentry at the gate, and the barracks for the guards couldn't hold more than fifteen men. There was another barracks for slaves of about the same size. We figure that's for the slaves kept alive to dig the pits."

"That's it? No one guarding the perimeter? No artillery?"

"The camp is so far out in the country, they must reckon they don't need it. We only found it so quickly because people had noticed the new railroad spur they laid to it."

"It's almost tempting to form a posse and go take care of this ourselves."

"And have every Confederate soldier in Alabama and Georgia come after us? I think we'd better leave this to men who are trained for it. And who are younger than us." Both men smiled. "Besides, that wouldn't stop the death riders. The Yankees need to know about them, too. They might be able to intercept them, because they appear to operate close to the front lines."

"Then what were they doing here?" Phil asked.

"That's just it. From what we know, I don't think your slaves were shot by a designated company of death riders. Rumor has it that all Rebel soldiers are now being encouraged to shoot slaves to prevent their liberation. Some of the boys coming through must have decided to interpret that loosely."

"So every day we delay, no telling how many more slaves will be killed," Phil said, nodding. "Okay, I'll leave for Chattanooga in the morning."

"And what story will you use to get through the lines?"

Phil paused. "I hadn't got that far. What do you recommend?"

Grady looked at him with a very serious expression on his face.

"I could be shot for what I'm about to do. You and I have known each other a long time, and we don't agree on everything. Can I trust you not to expose me?"

"It's a fair question," Phil said, "but you know where I stand. While I think the South is right, you'll recall that I thought secession to be a bad idea, one doomed to failure. Remember?"

"Yes, I remember you saying that."

"And while I believe slavery to be ordained by God, you also know I treat my slaves well. I would never advocate murdering anyone, slave or not. You know me well enough to know that." Grady nodded. "Anyway, the Confederacy has betrayed me, betrayed its own principles. So, yes, you can trust me."

Satisfied, Grady nodded again. Then, turning, he opened a small drawer in the table beside his chair and pulled out some papers.

"Here's a pass that will get you through the lines," he said, handing a folded paper to Phil. "And this is a letter addressed to you from a family member in Chattanooga, bearing the sad news that your elderly mother just passed away. That's your reason for traveling. When you get there, take the letter to the address at the top and ask for the person who sent it."

"And he'll be my contact?"

"He doesn't exist. It's a fake name. When you ask for him, they'll ask who you are. You will reply with your full name, but give 'Dexter' as your middle name. That will be their confirmation. They'll get you in to see the military leadership in Chattanooga."

Phil stood looking down at the papers, shaking his head and smiling.

"Never thought I'd be a spy," he said. "Especially for the North."

"Stranger things have happened these past four years."

Twelve days later, Grady Morrison heard another knock at his door. He opened it to see Phil Drinnon and his slave Dexter in the company of four Confederate soldiers.

"Come in," he said.

The men filed into the living room, where they took off their gloves and coats. The soldier wearing a corporal's insignia extended his hand to Grady.

"Mr. Morrison?"

"Yes."

"Is it safe to speak freely?"

"Yes, it is."

"I'm Lieutenant Sam Taylor, United States Army."

"Nice to meet you," Grady said. "Great job on the uniforms."

Lieutenant Taylor looked down at his clothes. "Thanks. We've fooled the Rebs so far."

"Here, let's sit around the table."

The group moved into the dining room, the wood floor creaking beneath the soldiers' boots. There was a pen and paper on the table. Grady took one of the sheets of paper, dipped the pen, and started drawing a map.

"You'll take the road to Anniston, and from there the road toward Columbus. Turn off at Foster's Crossroads, then turn here, and again here." As he spoke, he marked the roads on the map he was drawing. "When you get to this road, you'll see a little country church called Lightfoot Methodist. Up on a hill behind it is the church graveyard. At midnight on Thursday night, a slave named Alonzo will meet you there. He'll lead you to the camp."

"Looks simple enough," Lieutenant Taylor said.

"Simple to that point, but plenty dangerous after that," Grady said. He turned and spoke to Dexter. "Especially for you and Alonzo. They could shoot you on sight. Are you sure you want to do this?"

Instead of responding, Dexter reached up and pulled his shirt collar away from his shoulder, displaying a garish wound that was still scarring over. Grady looked at the wound, then at Dexter, and nodded.

"I understand. Well, God be with you. God be with you all."

Eight

LIBERATION

"SMELL'S COMING BACK," CAPTAIN SMITHSON said as he and his men lounged around in front of the camp barracks.

"Yep, spring is here," said one of four men playing cards around a tree stump.

"Well, somebody go tell the spear chuckers to spread a new layer of lime."

A man standing behind the card players nodded and turned toward the slave barracks. Just then they heard a voice hailing them from the woods. The men all jumped to their feet and looked in the direction of the shout. Several of them reached for their rifles. The man who had started toward the slave barracks took several quick steps and growled at the slaves lounging there.

"Get inside! Now!" They quickly obeyed.

"Halt!" cried the sentry at the front gate. "Who goes there?"

"Friend!" came the reply. "Delivering contraband."

"Show yourself!"

The sentry had aimed his rifle in the direction of the calls. The men in the camp all stood poised for action. Out of the trees rode four ragged Confederate soldiers. On a fifth horse were two slaves, their hands tied behind their backs.

Most of the men immediately relaxed and returned to their seats, while a few remained standing, rifles in hand.

"Just dropping off contraband on our way through," one of the soldiers on horseback called out. "More coming behind us."

They rode up to the entrance and stopped. The soldier who had spoken wore the insignia of a corporal. The sentry aimed away from the men but kept his rifle raised as Smithson strolled casually over, his hands behind his back.

"On your way through to where?" Smithson asked.

The soldiers had to assume the man addressing them was the commanding officer, even though he wore only an undershirt tucked into filthy pants. Something in his manner made it clear he didn't expect a salute.

"Anniston," replied the corporal. "They're combining regiments. We used to be with . . ."

"Yes, yes, very interesting," Smithson interrupted. "Just drop them off and we'll take care of them." Turning back toward the barracks, he said to the sentry, "Check their papers."

The soldiers glanced at each other.

"Uh, sir?"

"What?"

"Could we get some water for our horses, real quick-like?"

"Yeah, but real quick-like," Smithson said. As he rejoined his men, they leaned their guns against the barracks wall and turned back to watch the card game.

"Thanks," said the corporal.

He and his men dismounted and dragged the two slaves roughly from the saddle. Three of them led the horses to the trough inside the gate. The corporal pushed the two slaves through the gate, then pulled out a sheaf of papers. As the sentry examined the papers, the corporal leaned toward him and spoke under his breath.

"Hey, can I ask you something?"

"Sure."

"Do you think he'd mind if . . ."

"If what?"

"If we, uh, took care of these two? I been dyin' to kill me a nigger, and you guys get to do it all the time." The sentry smiled, then turned and shouted.

"Hey, Cap'n! Okay if they take care of these two?" Smithson replied with a dismissive wave of his hand.

The sentry handed the papers back and pointed toward the other end of the camp. One soldier stayed with the horses while the other three marched the bound slaves forward. When they passed the barracks and the lounging men, the corporal stopped and spoke.

"So, down the slope there?"

"Yep," said the man standing closest to them. Then he thought of something and turned toward them. "Hey, be sure you stand them on the very edge of the pit, or you'll have to pick them up and swing them into it. Bastards have a habit of falling straight down."

"Thanks. That's some mighty helpful advice," the corporal said. Lifting his rifle to his hip, he shot the man square in the chest. Simultaneously, the soldiers guarding the slaves lifted their rifles and killed two others. The sentry, who had turned his back on the soldier by the horses, received a point-blank shot to the back of the head.

But the real surprise was the two slaves. The ropes that appeared to bind them fell away, and when they brought their arms around, each hand held a cocked revolver that had been hidden in their trousers. Four more men fell dead, and before they hit the ground, the disguised Union soldiers had all drawn pistols.

"Hands in the air!" shouted Lieutenant Sam Taylor, United States Army. The stunned guards did as they were told, while the two slaves and the Union soldiers moved forward and collected their guns.

"Are there any more guards in the barracks?" Taylor asked. The remaining Rebels were frozen in surprise, but one or two slowly shook their heads. "Are there? Yes or no?"

"No sir," a young man said. "This is all of us."

Taylor swung his pistol over and aimed it directly at Smithson, then strode toward him menacingly. If Smithson was afraid, he didn't show it, maintaining the same look of disdain he always carried.

"Who's your superior officer?" Taylor demanded.

"McFall," came the clipped reply.

"What's his full name and rank?"

"Lieutenant Colonel Troy McFall."

"Who else is involved in this camp?"

"That's it; that's all I know. Just him and his aide, a kid named Henshaw."

"Where's he stationed?"

"Montgomery, last I heard. We don't keep in regular contact."

"What about the death riders going around killing slaves? Who's in charge of those?"

"I don't know anything about that."

"You don't know about the death riders?"

"First I've heard of them."

"Then you're of no more use to us." Without a second's pause, he shot Smithson between the eyes. The other guns exploded, as well, and five more men fell along with Smithson. The two remaining Rebels had only seconds to beg for their lives as the men switched to new weapons and fired again.

"Search the camp," Taylor said. The men spread out and confirmed that there were no other guards. The slave barracks was eerily silent. Taylor nodded at Dexter. "Go liberate your people." Dexter smiled. Taylor looked around and spoke to his men. "Let's liberate those three horses, too, and whatever provisions they can carry."

Calling out to the men in the slave barracks, Dexter opened the door and peeped inside. Frightened eyes looked back at him from the shadowy interior. He threw the door open, spread his arms, and said, "My brothers, you have been spared by the Lord!" The men, who had lived every day under threat of instant execution, took a few moments to fully realize they were safe. Once they did, there were shouts and hosannas. Dexter and Alonzo were lifted up and carried around the camp.

Soon the group was retracing its route through the woods, the freed slaves walking in front. Only two of the camp's horses were loaded with provisions, because the freed men insisted that Dexter and Alonzo, their liberators, each have his own horse. After they got underway, Lieutenant Taylor pulled up next to Dexter.

"You know this war is almost over, don't you? How does it feel to know you'll soon be free?"

To his surprise, Dexter just shrugged his shoulders.

"Ain't free yet. Don't know what it will bring."

"I understand. But at least you won't have to work so hard."

"Don't know nobody who don't work hard."

Taylor, who had also grown up on a farm, could only nod in agreement.

"What I mean is, you won't have to work all day while your master reaps the benefits."

"Never worked harder than he did."

Now Taylor was slightly frustrated.

"Okay. But wouldn't you rather work for yourself than for someone else?"

"Don't you work for someone else?"

"Well, yes, but they don't own me."

"Don't they?"

Taylor knitted his brow. Like many from the North, he had been filled with images of ignorant hillbillies, cruel slave masters, and tortured slaves worked to near starvation. Instead, he had seen farms that looked like the farms back home and a civilian population that was genteel despite its anger. If there was cruelty, it wasn't committed openly, and many of the poorer whites were dressed no better than the slaves. He had also expected to be greeted by hordes of grateful Negroes hailing the Union troops as liberators, but for now the slaves in Chattanooga were just keeping their heads down until their fate was decided by a conflict in which they had no say. Even so, he had expected the slaves to at least be excited about the *idea* of freedom.

"But surely freedom will be better than slavery," he said to Dexter. "I mean, when you're free, you'll finally get to go . . . To go . . ."

Dexter turned and looked at him.

"Where? I'll get to go where?"

Taylor, embarrassed, had no answer.

Nine

FOUND OUT

ON APRIL 2, 1865, RICHMOND FELL to Grant. On the very same day, Major General James H. Wilson broke through the Confederate defenses at Selma, fifty miles from Montgomery. Luckily for McFall and his young aide, Wilson stayed in Selma for more than a week, giving them time to destroy everything connected to the program of elimination. Messages were sent to the execution squads telling them to cease operations and blend into the nearest regiment. Orders were sent to dismantle the processing camp, burn the buildings, and tear up the railroad spur. Whether these messages got through, they had no way of knowing.

On April 9th, Lee surrendered to Grant at Appomattox. When Wilson marched into Montgomery three days later, the city was surrendered peacefully. McFall and Tommy, along with the other officers and staff stationed there, were captured and detained. Confined to quarters and guarded around the clock, they could only bide their time while the machinery of war ground slowly to a halt.

Word spread that everyone would be freed after a suitable amount of time, provided they signed a loyalty oath. But on the fourth day, Union soldiers came and got Tommy from his guarded room. They put him in leg irons, led him outside, and shoved him into the back of a prison wagon. Through the small barred window of the wagon, he saw them bring out Colonel McFall, also in leg irons, and shove him into the back of another wagon.

They had been found out.

Ten

ENTER GENERAL DICKINSON

"THANK GOD LINCOLN DIDN'T LIVE to see these," said Union general Walter Dickinson. Matthew Brady's glass plates were laid out on a long conference table. Dickinson walked down the table, looking at the sepia-tone images of shallow communal graves, rotting corpses lying in cotton fields, and pits full of tangled bodies surrounded by wire fencing. "Do we have a count?"

"It looks like it's going to be somewhere in the neighborhood of a quarter million," said a lieutenant. "Of course, we'll never know the exact number."

"It could have been much worse," said another officer. "Apparently they only started these atrocities in the last year."

"They originally wanted to ship all slaves to multiple death camps like this one, where they could be executed in secret. But they were afraid of resistance from the slave owners, and they just didn't have the resources or the time. So they ended up with half a dozen companies going from farm to farm, shooting slaves on the spot."

"The 'death riders'?"

"That's what the slaves called them, yes, sir."

Dickinson sighed, rubbing his forehead with his fingers.

"What were they thinking?" he said. He looked up in time to see two of his officers glance at each other. "Okay, okay, I know what they were thinking. But still, this?" He indicated the photos with a wave of his hand.

"Yes, sir," said one officer.

There was silence in the room for a moment.

"Has any of this leaked out to the press yet?"

"Not as far as we can tell. The death camp photos just arrived yesterday, and we confiscated them immediately. The other photos go back as far as last summer, but no one understood the implications until now. As soon as we did, we confiscated them all."

"Good," Dickinson said. "If this gets out, it will destroy Lincoln's dream of re-uniting this country. With him gone, the Radical Republicans are going to come down on the South hard enough as it is. This turns every Confederate officer into a war criminal, with years of public trials to prolong the agony. Do we know how far up this thing goes?"

"As far as we can tell, this was a program hatched by a group of mid-level officers and carried out without the knowledge or consent of the Confederate leadership. The people we've interrogated insist that Jefferson Davis and his cabinet knew nothing about it. And certainly General Lee didn't know."

"Do we have reason to suspect they're just protecting the leadership?"

"If I were in their shoes, I'd be more likely to blame the leadership to protect myself," one officer said.

"Good point. Well, that's good to know. Not that it will matter to the Radical Republicans. And can you imagine the reaction in Europe if they saw these photos? People over there are already horrified by the slaughter of brother by brother in this war. This would make America absolutely abhorrent in the eyes of the world."

"Yes, sir," the officers agreed.

Dickinson stood with his hands on his hips, still looking at the photos.

"Well, we have to clamp down on this, and we have to do it now." He nodded at two of his officers. "Find Brady and his helpers and confiscate any other photos like these. Find out whether they've distributed any and track those down. If the newspapers know about this program, stop them from publishing anything about it. If they've made woodcuts based on these photos, confiscate those. Shut them down if you have to—this is a matter of national security. Take all the men you need. This has to be done quickly."

"Yes, sir," the men said, saluting and then heading out the door.

Dickinson spoke to those remaining. "I want all the Rebels who were involved in this to be brought here. We'll conduct their trials in absolute secrecy."

"Military trials, sir?"

"Yes, military tribunals." He paused, seeing the doubt on their faces. "What?"

"It's just that, well, the president is a Southerner," one soldier said hesitantly. "Do you think he'll authorize . . . ?"

"The president isn't going to know about it," Dickinson interrupted, "just as their president didn't know they were committing war crimes. Let me remind you that these are enemy combatants, captured on American soil. They may not have recognized it as

American soil, but it is and always has been. That's what this war was about."

"Yes, sir," one officer said, "but . . ."

"But what?"

"Well, sir, they weren't fighting us, and they weren't killing our civilians. They were just killing their own slaves."

"Well, slaves are civilians, aren't they? At least they were after the Emancipation Proclamation. These rebels were murdering free civilians. Right?"

"Yes, sir," one of the officers said, but without conviction.

"Are you suggesting we should just let these men go? You yourself referred to these killings as atrocities. Come on, speak freely."

"No, sir, not suggesting that at all, sir. These are absolutely atrocities. We were only concerned about how some people might view the use of secret military tribunals. The Northern Democrats who opposed the war already think Lincoln was a war criminal."

"And I'm supposed to care what a bunch of bleeding heart peacemongers think?"

"No, sir, but they could make a big deal out of it if word got out. The newspapers would have a field day with it."

Dickinson nodded, then stood thinking for a moment.

"Well, the way I see it, we have two choices: We can try these men in secret under military tribunals, or we can let them undergo public trials in civilian courts accompanied by an atmosphere of hysteria fueled by the newspapers and these photos. You tell me which courts are more likely to hand down the harsher sentences and execute the most people. The public and the Radical Republicans would feed on this for years. We'd have a decade of war crimes trials exposing every dirty deed committed throughout this war, all plastered across the front pages of newspapers around the world. Am I wrong?" He looked from one man to the other.

"No, sir," they said.

"Then we're agreed. Find these men and bring them here. This whole process needs to happen quickly, before the outside world catches on. If anyone asks you what you're doing, just refer them to me."

"Yes, sir."

"Do we know who the ringleaders are?"

"We just captured the top man."

"Who is he?"

"A Lieutenant Colonel Troy McFall, sir."

Dickinson pursed his lips. "I see. Let me know as soon as he arrives. That will be all."

As the men exited, one said to another, "That's going to be tough on the general."

"What is?"

"You don't know? McFall was his roommate at West Point."

Eleven

THE DEBATE

FTER AN ARDUOUS JOURNEY BY wagon and rail, Tommy was unloaded in the gray stone courtyard of a prison and led to a cell. His cellmate introduced himself as Ben Sanders, a name Tommy recognized from the payroll list of Captain Matthews's company. Tommy had never actually spoken with a member of an execution squad before, and he was anxious to hear about their experiences first-hand. However, he had barely cleaned up from his journey when the Yankee soldiers came back for him.

They led him down stark corridors into the prison mess hall, which was lit by high windows facing into the courtyard. The room was empty except for two more guards and Colonel McFall, who sat at one of the long wooden tables. He stood up when Tommy entered. As they approached each other, the colonel reached out and grasped his arms.

"I didn't tell them anything," Tommy blurted out. McFall smiled and shook his head to signify that it didn't matter.

"We may not have but a minute, so I want you listen to me," he said, looking his young aide in the eye. "You didn't do anything wrong, do you hear me? Don't ever feel guilty about anything you've done. As I said when we started, nothing happened because you were involved that wouldn't have happened anyway. Do you understand that?"

"Yes, sir," Tommy said, a little taken aback by his boss's intensity.

"Now look, I won't make it out of here alive, but you might. Give them your full cooperation. Sign whatever they ask you to sign—a loyalty oath, a confession, whatever. There's no honor in being a martyr to a lost cause. Got it?"

"Yes, sir."

"Good. Good." McFall looked at his young aide with a smile. "You've done a fine job. I wish you a long and prosperous life."

Tommy realized his C. O. was saying goodbye. He shuddered a bit inside. From the moment they were captured, he had taken it for granted that they might be executed, but now he realized how likely it was, and how quickly it might happen. He was only twenty-one years old.

They sat down together and waited. A few minutes later, the door opened and McFall's old West Point roommate walked in. They had both started to rise when Tommy was surprised by an outburst from his boss.

"Don't come in here giving me that look!" McFall shouted at Dickinson. "We only did what we had to do! The blood of the slaves we killed is on *your* hands!" He jabbed the air with his finger.

Dickinson had entered with a look of disappointment on his face, a look clearly meant as a silent reproach to his old classmate for his participation in the program of elimination. He was carrying under his arm a folder full of papers and several of the Brady plates, evidence he was planning to present in a preliminary enactment of McFall's upcoming trial. But McFall, being an astute observer of human nature, recognized all this in an instant. The anger behind his outburst was real, but Tommy knew his boss well enough to know that it was also a strategic ploy to put Dickinson on the defensive. And it worked. General Dickinson stopped in his tracks, as surprised by Colonel McFall's outburst as Tommy had been.

"*Our* hands? How could it possibly be on our hands?" And with that, Dickinson inadvertently allowed his prisoner to assume the role of prosecutor.

"You started arming our slaves against us," McFall said forcibly. "That made every slave a potential enemy combatant. We had no choice but to eliminate the threat. Doing so was a military necessity, one caused by your president's own proclamation."

Dickinson, setting his parcels on the table, surprised them by nodding his head. "Actually, I always said Lincoln erred in announcing that freed slaves would be armed for combat. Even if he was going to do so, he shouldn't have announced it publicly. But that doesn't make what you did okay. These were unarmed, innocent people."

"People? That's not how the United States Army treated them. The official position of the federal government is that the slaves were 'contraband,' property to be seized. Well, there's nothing wrong about disposing of one's property as one sees fit, is there? You can't say they're property one minute and people the next, just to suit your purposes."

"Oh no? Isn't that what the South did when the Constitution was being written? You say slaves are property, but you insisted they be counted in the census so you could have more representatives in Congress. The census counts people, not property."

"We did that because we needed to balance the anti-slavery forces in the North. Which is the same reason we needed new slave states. Without that balance, we knew the North would outlaw slavery. Kinda looks like we were right, doesn't it?"

"The balance wasn't maintained because our population grew faster than yours, and your own slave system is to blame for that. Unskilled immigrants looking for jobs can't compete with slave labor, so they stayed up north or headed west. You created the situation that gave the North the population to outvote you."

"But that's just it," McFall said. "The North didn't outvote us. They didn't amend the Constitution or defeat the Fugitive Slave Act. They didn't abide by the democratic process."

"When the South seceded, there was no immediate danger of slavery being outlawed, so don't pretend like you would have stuck around for a vote on it. Or that you would have abided by the results. You just said you were worried about the North having enough votes to outlaw slavery through the democratic process. That's why you left."

"We left because your side started breaking the law and violating the Constitution. Your own Supreme Court upheld the Fugitive Slave Act and ruled that Congress couldn't outlaw slavery in the territories. It wasn't the South that rebelled against that decision; it was the abolitionists."

"The *Dred Scott* decision itself violated the Constitution, which clearly states that Congress has the authority to regulate the territories. And there is no basis in the Constitution for the Court's declaration that even free Negroes have no rights. That wasn't the issue, and no one asked them to rule on that. They created a new constitutional policy out of thin air, with nothing in the Constitution to support it. It was blatant judicial activism, in which the Court usurped the role of Congress. When you take an issue out of the democratic process like that, the only option the people have left is civil disobedience."

"And if the Court had ruled the opposite—that slavery in the territories was unconstitutional—the abolitionists wouldn't have had the slightest complaint about this so-called 'judicial activism.'"

"No, but your side would have."

This resulted in a pause. Tommy realized he had completely forgotten his own predicament and become absorbed in the back-and-forth between these two men.

"In any case," said McFall, "the South joined the United States only after making sure slavery would be allowed under the Constitution. That was the agreement that got us into the union."

"The Founding Fathers agreed to allow slavery where it existed. Nothing was ever said about letting it spread."

"And nothing was ever said about the union being permanent, either. There's nothing in the Constitution that says a state can't leave if it wants to. You call us traitors, but where exactly did we violate the Constitution? Point out the specific passage to me. You can't, because it isn't there. And do you know why it isn't there? Because the Founding Fathers themselves couldn't agree on whether the union was permanent."

"And yet the South's own Andrew Jackson threatened to hang secessionists from the nearest tree and declared 'Our union—it must be preserved!' Obviously he believed secession to be treason."

"Yes, and there have been plenty of Northerners—from John Quincy Adams to Horace Greeley—who have believed secession to be perfectly legal. Jackson had a right to his opinion, but there's nothing in the Constitution to back it up. The whole point of having a constitution is so the country will be ruled by law and not by opinion. Isn't that what you were just complaining about in the *Dred Scott* decision?"

"Even if secession were legal, you couldn't make that decision unilaterally. Congress has the power to admit new states, so Congress would have to vote to let states leave."

"The Constitution doesn't say that!" McFall shouted. "There's no law that says that! That's just your opinion! And you *murdered* people based on your opinion."

McFall said the word "murdered" with real venom, jabbing his finger toward Dickinson's chest. Tommy glanced at the sentries by the door and saw them stiffen. But then McFall stepped back, looked down, and shook his head.

"And you have the nerve to call us traitors," he continued, still shaking his head. "We may be rebels, but we're not traitors. We didn't violate the Constitution. We didn't try to overthrow the government of the United States. We didn't betray it to a foreign power. We didn't try to capture U. S. territory. We didn't try to harm the remaining states or the bond they share. We just wanted to leave."

"You wanted to leave and take federal property with you— our forts and other installations. That's U. S. territory."

"That doesn't wash and you know it. The federal government only had that land because the states gave it to them. Once the contract that formed the union was voided, that land naturally reverted back to the states. Besides, if you were only concerned about the federal property we took, you would have just tried to recapture that property, not conquer the entire South." Dickinson started to speak, but McFall didn't let him. "When America rebelled against the British, you took all their government property, didn't you? Your great uncle fought in the Revolutionary War—was he a traitor?" Dickinson just shrugged his shoulders. "Well, was he or wasn't he? Because if I'm a traitor, then so was he. If we're traitors, then America was founded by traitors."

"Okay, fine, so you're rebels and not traitors," Dickinson said. "Now let's talk about your own rhetoric. You like to call this 'the War of Northern Aggression,' but you fired the first shot. You fired on a federal fort, for God's sake. You bombarded it for hours before anyone had fired a shot at you. You initiated hostilities. I've never understood that, from a tactical standpoint or a public relations standpoint. Why didn't you wait and force Lincoln to fire on you first? Then maybe you could have positioned yourself in the eyes of the world as the victims in this whole thing. Have you forgotten the symbolic importance of the Boston Massacre?"

Now it was Dickinson's turn to be surprised, because McFall nodded as he spoke.

"You're right about that. I have to agree with that. When I first heard the news from Charleston, I thought exactly the same thing. It was a huge blunder." McFall paused as he mused on the strategic mistakes made by his side, mistakes he was sure had cost the South the war.

"Look, we've heard all these arguments before," Dickinson said. "Why don't we just agree to disagree?" But this got McFall started again.

"That's what we tried to do! The North and South disagreed, so we tried to leave. But you wouldn't let us. If your business partner disagrees with you and wants to leave the business, are you going to force him to stay in the business against his will? If a woman hates you and doesn't want to be with you, are you going to kidnap her and force her to marry you anyway, like some Arabian sheik? Your side has acted like a man who'd rather kill his sweetheart than let her go. Who gave you the authority to tell other people what to do and where to live? Who made you the kings of the world? If you're against involuntary bondage, why are you keeping us where we don't want to be?"

Dickinson raised his palms in acquiescence. "All right, fine. It won't do any good to jump all over me. I can't undo the war."

"No, but you can admit your actions are hypocritical and your arguments inconsistent. You said we couldn't secede from the union, even though the Constitution doesn't say that. Then you turned right around and let West Virginia secede from Virginia, even though the Constitution specifically prohibits forming a new state from an old one without the approval of the legislature. You accuse us of violating the Constitution even as you violate it yourselves."

"Virginia had already seceded when West Virginia was formed, so it can hardly appeal to the Constitution."

"Not according to Lincoln! Lincoln's position was that the Confederate states never left the union, that the Constitution always applied to them. Yet it was he who accepted the illegal statehood of West Virginia." He paused and looked meaningfully at Dickinson. "If the Constitution applied to the South during the war, West Virginia should be restored to Virginia. If it didn't, then what we did to our slaves is none of your business, and you should let us all go. Which is it?"

Dickinson involuntarily averted his eyes. Only days before, he had told his own officers that the Constitution had always applied to the South. While McFall didn't know this, he could tell he had made his point. He wagged his finger at Dickinson.

"You use whichever argument serves your purpose at the moment. You told us we couldn't leave the union, but now you're setting conditions for our 'readmission.' You were just complaining about our taking federal property, but you took our slaves, and now your General Sherman is taking our land. He's taking our land and giving it to our slaves with no due process, no legislative approval, no legal authority whatsoever."

Dickinson raised one eyebrow. The edges of his mouth curled into a sly smile. "So you're against military officers acting under their own authority, are you?"

McFall had already opened his mouth to continue when he saw Dickinson's expression and realized the point he was making. His mouth closed halfway. Try as he might, he couldn't stop himself from smiling. He even let out a chuckle.

"*Touché*," he said. He looked down and shook his head, still smiling sheepishly. "*Touché*."

And with that, the tension was broken.

"Why don't we sit down?" Dickinson suggested with a smile. McFall and Tommy nodded and took their seats. "I think we're both guilty of using whichever argument benefits us at the moment. Perhaps we should just admit that there were plenty of mistakes made on both sides."

"Oh, sure, but the North will never admit it," McFall said, though without the same fire in his voice. "You'll position yourselves as the defenders of all that is holy, and you'll teach our own grandchildren that we were traitors with purely evil motives. And you'll use slavery—the one thing this war was supposedly *not* about—as your weapon. Meanwhile, you've got ten-year-old kids working twelve-hour shifts in your factories. Be sure to put *that* into the history books."

Dickinson waited to see if McFall would say anything else, then spoke in a quiet voice. "Look, Troy, I didn't mean to come across as judgmental when I came in. I knew you before the war, and I know you to be an honorable man. I know you wouldn't hurt anyone without feeling that you had to. But surely you understand how this looks to people. Surely you knew when you started that this would . . ."

"Yes, of course I knew," McFall said, cutting him off. "But we had no choice. We did what we had to do."

Dickinson nodded. After another pause, he put his hand on the table near McFall's arm, but without actually touching him. "I understand your reasoning behind what you did. But you understand there's nothing I can do to save you, don't you?"

"Yes, I understand." All three men looked down at the table in silence. Then McFall spoke again. "There is one favor I'd like to ask, though."

"What's that?"

He nodded his head sideways in the direction of Tommy.

"The boy here is innocent. He was my aide before we started the program, and all he did was follow orders. He's got his whole life ahead of him. If you're inclined to fulfill a doomed man's last request, you'll let him go home."

Without realizing it, Tommy held his breath waiting for the answer.

"Actually, I can fulfill that request, but I'll need two things in return." Dickinson was still speaking to McFall, not to Tommy.

"What's that?"

"First, you sign a confession and waive your right to a trial. If you'll do that, the official cause of death will be illness while on active duty. Your name won't be connected with this program, and if there's ever any pension money for Confederate soldiers, your family will be able to get it."

"I don't want you sticking your neck out for me."

"I'm not doing it for you. I'm doing it to cover up the existence of this program. If this gets out, it will just make things worse for everybody, especially the South."

"Fair enough," McFall said, nodding. "What else?"

"I just need some information from the two of you. As you know, we've already captured one of the companies you had killing slaves, and they face execution just as you do. As far as we can tell, they don't know the identities of the members of the other squads. You two are the only ones who can tell us that."

Tommy rose quickly from his seat. "Give up the lives of dozens of other men just to save my own? You can forget it!" But Dickinson had already raised his hand to calm him.

"You won't be giving up anyone's life," he said. "We have another reason for finding these men. Let me explain."

Tommy sat down slowly. The three men talked a while longer.

The room was growing dark as dusk approached, so Dickinson called in his aide and asked for candles. He also told him to see if the warden had any whiskey. When the aide returned with the requested items, Dickinson said goodbye to Tommy and told the guards to return him to his cell. As the mess hall door swung shut, Tommy looked back to see the two former roommates drinking a toast, illuminated only by candlelight. They had been friends, then mortal enemies, and one was about to have the other executed, yet here they were, sharing a glass of whiskey and reminiscing about their days at West Point. Such was the nature of this strangest of all wars.

When he got back to his cell, he found that Ben Sanders didn't need much prompting to start talking about his experiences with the execution squad. He was especially proud of the time he pretended to be a Union messenger and fooled the Yankees into running off to a fictitious battle. He laughed at how they surprised the freed slaves before shooting them and pushing them over the side of the road into a ravine.

This was the first time Tommy had heard details of the killings. The program of elimination had been, for him, mainly a matter of forms to be filled out and sent off—payroll vouchers, supply requisitions. Even though he knew what the program entailed, his only contact with the men involved had been when the camp was being set up. As his boss had promised, he had never seen a slave killed. Now, sitting on his bunk in that dark cell, he listened as Ben recounted one killing after another, all in a voice that wasn't exactly disinterested, but that held no hint of concern for the human suffering it was reporting.

While they were talking, they heard footsteps and saw torchlight approaching. To Tommy's surprise, General Dickinson came to his cell, still holding his packet of materials under his arm. He handed Tommy one of the bulky glass photographic plates and nodded at the guard to hold the torch so he could see it.

"Your C. O. will be hanged in the morning, so there's no reason to make him look at these," Dickinson said. "But before we let you go, I want you to see your handiwork."

Tommy looked down and saw an image that didn't make sense. It looked like the pieces of a puzzle spread out on a table, with arms and legs and heads and torsos, but all mixed up. Then the image coalesced into a large pit full of bodies, frozen at odd angles by *rigor mortis* and covered by a deathly white hue of lime.

"That's one of three pits at your death camp," Dickinson said. He took the picture back and handed him one that showed rotting bodies lying between rows of cotton, their half-full pick sacks still around their shoulders. A third photograph showed more swollen corpses on the ground, but this time they were white men.

"Recognize this?" Dickinson asked. Tommy shook his head dumbly. "Those are the guards at your death camp. The camp was reported to Union troops by Southern civilians whose slaves you had killed."

Several other photos followed. After he took the last one back, Dickinson put his hand on Tommy's shoulder. "I'm sure you're a fine boy, and I'm sure you never hurt a fly prior to this war. I'm sure you'll never hurt anyone again. But I wanted you to see what you had done. I wanted you to understand why you're under a death sentence. I hope you take it seriously."

"Yes, sir," Tommy mumbled, looking down. As Dickinson turned to go, Ben, who had watched the proceedings from his bunk, spoke up.

"Are those pictures any worse than the pictures of the Rebels you gunned down on their own farms and in their own towns?

Well, are they?" Neither Dickinson nor the guard responded
as they walked away. Ben stood up and walked to the cell door.
"What about *our* deaths?" he shouted at the receding torchlight.
"Don't our deaths matter? Who's going to hang for our deaths?"
With a dismissive grunt he turned and kicked at the floor. He
dropped back onto his bunk, muttering "goddamn Yankees" as he
did. Then, after a pause, he said, "Don't let 'em get to ya, kid."

"I won't," Tommy replied. But as he lay in his bunk staring
at the stone ceiling, he realized for the first time the savagery of
what they had done. In the end, like the rebellion itself, it had all
been for naught. All those lives lost, and for what? His boss would
be executed in the morning, and he had barely escaped the noose
himself. The relief, the horror, the futility, and a dozen other
thoughts and emotions, many of them held in check since the
war began, now impressed themselves upon him. Tears streamed
down his temples into his ears as he lay silently crying, alternately
thanking God, asking His forgiveness, and, as always, cursing
the North.

Twelve

THE GALLOWS

THE NEXT MORNING AT SUNRISE, Tommy stood in the courtyard while Lieutenant Colonel Troy E. McFall, C. S. A., climbed the steps of the wooden scaffold. Tommy had been made to sign a loyalty oath, as well as an oath of silence about the program of elimination. It was stressed to him that he was on lifelong probation—one word to anyone about the program could result in life imprisonment or even summary execution. To ensure that he took the situation seriously, he was made to stay and watch as his C. O. was hanged.

Before the rope was placed around McFall's neck, he was asked if he had any last words. He took a step forward. Tommy, General Dickinson, and a small guard of Union soldiers were the only ones present in the courtyard, but the Confederate prisoners whose cell windows opened onto the courtyard could also observe the proceedings. McFall, the West Point professor of military history now giving his last lecture, lifted his chin and spoke loudly enough for everyone to hear.

"'We hold these truths to be self-evident, that all men are created equal, that they are endowed by their Creator with certain unalienable rights, that among these are life, liberty and the pursuit of happiness.'"

Dickinson wondered for a moment if McFall was going to acknowledge the slaves' right to freedom. Instead, McFall lowered his head and looked directly at his old West Point roommate. He continued, emphasizing certain words.

""That to secure these rights, governments are instituted among men, deriving their just powers from the *consent of the governed.*'" He spoke these last four words separately and distinctly. ""That whenever any form of government becomes destructive of these ends, it is the *right of the people* to *alter* or to *abolish* it, and to institute new government, laying its foundation on such principles and organizing its powers in such form, as *to them* shall seem most likely to effect their safety and happiness.'"

He paused. The Confederate prisoners who could hear him from their cells burst into applause. Dickinson was relieved when McFall finally looked away from him.

"Those are the words that justified the separation of the American colonies from England," McFall continued. "Relying on those sacred truths, the colonies took up arms against their former countrymen and ran them off their territory. Just three generations later, we attempted to do exactly the same thing. What has been our reward? To be branded traitors by the same government that celebrates its own treason every July 4th. To be slaughtered unmercifully by the government that claims to believe in life and liberty. To be forced to remain under the control of a government whose entire *raison d'être* is that no man should be forced to remain under the control of any government. Your hypocrisy could not be more profound."

He addressed this last sentence once again to Dickinson. Then he continued.

"The abolitionists focus exclusively on the statement that all men are created equal, insisting that slavery violates this principle. Abraham Lincoln used this argument throughout his debates with Douglas. But what about the rest of the passage? What about the right to alter or abolish our government? Are we to place such heavy emphasis on one phrase that we will slaughter our own countrymen over it, yet ignore the entire rest of the passage? Are we to guarantee liberty to slaves at the price of withdrawing it from free men? If slavery is evil, surely murder is more so. Forcing us to stay in the union clashes with the American ideal of liberty at least as much as the practice of slavery clashes with the American ideal of equality. Even if we're both wrong, you are guilty of a hypocrisy that undermines the very foundation of America, for you have taken up arms against those who attempted to live out the ideals that justified your own independence.

"Mark that down: The Declaration of Independence has now been invalidated by the United States government. In America, you do NOT have the right to 'dissolve the political bands' that tie you to others. In America, you do NOT have the right 'to assume among the powers of the earth, the separate and equal station to which the Laws of Nature and of Nature's God entitle' you. In America, 'whenever any Form of Government becomes destructive of these ends,' it is NOT your right 'to throw off such Government.' The words of the Declaration of Independence no longer apply to the United States of America, and July 4th should never again be celebrated as this nation's birthday." The Rebel soldiers cheered from their cells again.

"Now let me give you another quotation. See if you can guess who said this: 'Any people anywhere, being inclined and having the power, have the right to rise up and shake off the existing government, and form a new one that suits them better. This is a most valuable, a most sacred right—a right which, we hope and believe, is to liberate the world.' Abraham Lincoln spoke those words in 1848 as a member of Congress, when he opposed the war with Mexico. What can you say about a man who cites a principle while in Congress and then tramples on that principle when he's president? I would say he's a man without principles. But what do you expect when you elect a man president after only one term in Congress?

"President Lincoln didn't believe Negroes to be equal to whites, and your own General Sherman doesn't believe it. Yet these men were willing to wage war, even against civilians, in order to keep us in the union. If they didn't believe Negroes to be our equal, they could only have been fighting to keep us under their control. This war was not about freeing men in bondage; it was about keeping free men in bondage.

"The Confederacy never intended to be the enemy of the United States. We just wanted to leave and form our own nation, in accordance with the principles set forth in the Declaration of Independence. Once we formed our own nation, we had every intention of being allies and trading partners with the United States. We didn't want to fight the United States; we only did that because the United States sent troops to stop us from leaving. Forcing us to fight and then condemning us as traitors is hardly fair.

"What is most amazing to me is that the North allowed itself to be drawn into this bloody and illegal war by an inexperienced president who was elected without a majority, and by a brand new, one-issue political party that exists solely to impose its moral and religious views on others.

"In the months leading up to Fort Sumter, proposal after proposal was introduced to Congress in an attempt to achieve compromise and avoid secession. These proposals came from Northerners as well as Southerners, from Whigs as well as Democrats, but every one of them failed because the Republicans voted against them. Time after time they said no, while offering no productive ideas of their own. They said no to the Crittenden Compromise. They said no to the proposals of the Washington Peace Conference. They said no to the Corwin Amendment, even though what it proposed was in their own party platform!

"The Republican message to the South was no, you can't own slaves, even though the Constitution says you can, and no, you can't leave the union, even though the Declaration of Independence says you can. The Republican Party may as well be called 'the Party of No,' because that's all they know how to do. Yet you allowed them to send your sons off to die by the thousands.

"In the end, we'll all pay the price. Having established, at the point of a gun, that no one is allowed to leave this nation under any circumstances—having revoked the right to rebel that was, until this moment, enshrined in the Declaration of Independence—the federal government will now feel emboldened to expand its power over everyone and everything it pleases. Henceforth, every generation will feel itself further under the heel of government control. That is the history of governments throughout human history, and the result is always tyranny."

McFall looked down and addressed himself to the Union soldiers standing below him. "You think you've freed the slaves, but what you've really done is initiate a chain of events that will enslave you all. You think you've saved the union, but what you've really done is start the process that will someday destroy this nation. Let me tell you how it will happen:

"Four years ago, for the first time in American history, the federal government imposed a tax on incomes to help fund this misguided war. You remember how the tax was sold on the grounds that it would only apply to the rich? Do you remember that the very next year they lowered the threshold and raised the rate? Then just last year they raised the rate again, doubling it for most people. Do you remember that? Do you remember that they also sold this as a temporary measure? Now that the war is over, do you really think this tax will go away? If so, you're all fools. You'll be paying an income tax every year for the rest of your lives, and it will increase steadily, bit by bit, for every generation.

"Here's another example: Every one of you is a citizen of a state as well as of this nation. The Tenth Amendment specifically protects the rights of the states, and of the people, against encroachment by the federal government. In addition, Article Four of the Constitution guarantees a republican form of government. But now the idea of states' rights is sneered at, and you can expect those rights to be eroded steadily in the future. You may laugh about it now, but it will affect you and your progeny for the rest of this country's future as power is slowly concentrated in the hands of the few.

"Third, the U. S. Constitution provides for slavery. It also states, and I quote, 'nor shall any person be deprived of life, liberty, *or property* without due process of law, nor shall private property be taken for public use, without just compensation.'

Where was the due process for taking away our slaves? Where was the compensation? We received neither. And what was the government's justification for depriving us of those constitutional rights? Why, that we were in the act of trying to stop them from depriving us of our rights! There's the new governing principle of the United States: They can take away your rights, and if you try to stop them, your resistance will merely justify their actions. If that isn't the logic of tyranny, I don't know what is.

"Finally, you'll notice that the federal government used a military crisis to take away our rights and to impose new controls. Now that the crisis is ending, will those rights be returned, those controls relaxed? Of course not. That's the way it's always done. Every loss of liberty is precipitated by some crisis, real or imagined. A riot is an excuse to take away your right to assemble. An economic crisis is an excuse to expand control over commerce. The acts of criminals are used to take away the rights of the law-abiding. Every little problem is an excuse to introduce further regulations, but those regulations never seem to quite solve the problem, so still more regulations are needed. Eventually the government collapses under its own weight, and a dictator steps in to fill the gap. It's happened throughout human history, and it will happen in America. The only question is when.

"As for me, I'm being executed for trying to solve a problem created by the North. We were forced to do what we did by the illegal and immoral decision to free our slaves and arm them against us. What we did, we did out of military necessity. Anyone in our situation would have done the same. The North is complicit in this, which is precisely why you are hanging me. You'll kill me, then you'll write the history books to make the South the only villain in this whole sorry episode. You'll make slavery the only issue so you won't have to acknowledge all the other issues. You'll do this because we were guilty of the slavery issue, but you're guilty of all the others.

"But no matter how you write the history books, it won't change the reality now facing this nation. Overnight, your carelessness and your hypocrisy have created a subclass of Americans who move in your midst with no skills, no jobs, no land, no direction, and no friends. Marked by their skin color, they will be unable to assimilate. Only a fool would fail to see that this is a powder keg waiting to ignite."

Then Colonel McFall spoke his final words:

"I predict that this country will be dealing with racial issues one hundred years in the future, or longer."

Thirteen

REPRIEVE

CAPTAIN MATTHEWS AND HIS MEN sat listlessly around the tables in the prison mess hall, wondering why they were there. One man was slowly chewing tobacco, occasionally dribbling black juice into a tin can. The squad had been captured by General Wilson's forces as he swept down through Mississippi and Alabama on his way to Selma and Montgomery. The Union troops soon realized these were the men responsible for the communal graves they kept running across, and when they did, the company was shipped north by rail. That morning they had watched the hanging of Colonel McFall from their cell windows.

The door opened and in strode a flamboyantly dressed Union cavalry officer with blue eyes and long, curly, reddish-blond hair. Although boyish in appearance, he wore the insignia of a major general. He stopped and stood cockily, his elbow resting on the handle of his saber, and looked from man to man. It became apparent that he was expecting some sign of recognition, but all he got were stares of indifference and derision.

"Do any of you know who I am?" he asked.

"A sissy?" asked Ben Sanders.

The whole group broke into laughter.

"A preening dandy?" said someone else. More laughter. The officer's blue eyes flashed with anger for a second, but he caught himself and gave a self-deprecating smile.

"Okay, okay," he said. "I deserved that. Allow me to introduce myself."

""Wait, wait," Ben said, still laughing. "Don't we get three guesses?" The men laughed at this, as well.

"Okay, you guys, that's enough," Captain Matthews said. "Settle down." Turning to the officer, he said, "You'll have to forgive them, General. You see, we figure we'll be swinging from ropes in the courtyard ourselves pretty soon, so we don't really have a lot of interest in what anyone has to say to us."

"Which is precisely why you should be interested in what I have to say. I can save you from the gallows." At this, the laughter died away. "I've come to offer you a bargain."

"Go on, General Custer," said Matthews.

"Ah, so you do know who I am."

"Yes, we know," Matthews said, uncomfortable with feeding Custer's ego.

"Yeah," said Ben. "Who doesn't know the famed George Armstrong Custer?" Custer smiled at this, but Ben wasn't through. "General Custer, the man who led the charge at Bull Run . . . back to Washington!" The men around him laughed. "The officer who lost more men than any other brigade at Gettysburg. The only Union officer to have his underwear captured . . . without him in it!" The group erupted once again. Custer's smile had diminished with each sentence.

"Hey, Ben," called out another man. "What do they call a man who graduates last in his class at West Point?"

"I don't know, Jake. What do they call a man who graduates last in his class at West Point?"

"General Custer!"

The group roared. One of the guards at the door stepped forward to restore order, but Custer waved him back. Captain Matthews and Lieutenant Watkins motioned for their men to calm down, but to no avail. There was nothing to do but let the laughter run its course. As it finally began to subside, Custer dipped his head and strolled casually toward the wall with the high windows.

"Quite right, gentlemen, quite right. I did indeed graduate last in my class at West Point. I then led the attack that captured the first Confederate battle flag of the war." This statement caused the laughter to cease, freezing the men's smiles on their faces. Custer wheeled around on one heel and started strolling in the opposite direction.

"And yes, I did indeed lose more men at Gettysburg than anyone else. And had my horse shot out from under me," he added for emphasis. "It was the price I paid to defeat your General Jeb Stuart. Which left Pickett's Charge without cavalry support. And cost you the battle." The Confederates had stopped smiling. Custer wheeled around once again.

"And yes, it's true that my personal belongings were captured along with my supply train during the Overland Campaign. But it's also true that my division blocked Lee's retreat on the last day of the war and received his flag of truce. Perhaps that's why the table upon which the truce was signed at Appomattox is now being shipped to my home. Where it will sit in my parlor. As a souvenir."

Custer stopped and stood at the spot where he had begun. The men were now silent, staring angrily at the floor.

"Okay, General," said Matthews, "you've made your point. Let's move on. You said something about a bargain?"

"I ain't interested in no bargain from this scalawag!" Ben shouted, jumping to his feet. But Matthews, without turning his head, shouted just as loudly.

"You gave him guff and he gave it back! So take it!" Ben glared at Matthews but said nothing. Matthews turned in his seat to look at him. "The man said he can save us from the gallows. If you're not interested, go back to your cell. I'm bettin' the rest of us want to hear what he has to say."

Ben sat down grudgingly. Everyone turned back to Custer.

"Thank you, Captain. As you know, gentlemen, the settlement of the West, our Manifest Destiny, has been continuing even with the war going on. Now, with the war ended and the slavery issue settled, thousands are poised to head west in search of free land and wide open spaces. It's time to bring civilization to the rest of America. There's only one thing standing in our way, and that's the Indians.

"I've been ordered west to head up the U. S. 7th Cavalry at Fort Riley, Kansas. I'll be supporting General Winfield Scott Hancock's campaign against the Cheyenne. Let me make it clear that we will not be playing nursemaid to settlers. Our job is to remove the threat. Those Indians who will move peacefully to reservations will do so. The rest we will eliminate. So, as you can see, we have need of men with your particular, shall we say, talents and experience."

He paused. The men looked at each other. Not surprisingly, Ben was the first to speak.

"Let me get this straight," he said. "You're going to hang us for killing Negras, but you'll pay us to kill Indians?"

"That is correct. Fulfill a four-year enlistment with me and you'll receive a full pardon and an army pension. How long has it been since you men were paid?"

"Four months," Matthews said.

"Fine. Join me and I'll throw in four months' pay as a signing bonus."

But Ben wasn't through. He shook his head in an exaggerated manner, as if trying to clear it. "Okay, so, wait. I just want to make sure I've got this straight. The Negras—who were savages over in Africa—you've freed them, and you're probably going to make them American citizens. But the Indians, who are savages here, you're going to eliminate. And you don't see a problem with that?"

"I don't make policy, gentlemen. I fight wars."

"Well, I just want to make my point, which is that what you're doing to the Indians justifies what we were doing to the Negras. If what you're doing is right, then what we were doing is right."

"Nevertheless, your choices are to join me or hang. I'll give you until tomorrow morning to decide." Custer removed his hat and gave a sweeping bow. Then he turned and departed.

Ben shook his head. "Geez, and they wonder why we wanted to leave their screwed-up country."

No one said anything for a moment.

"Okay," said Matthews. "So what are we going to do?"

"Well, I guess we're going out west to kill Indians," said Lieutenant Watkins. Several heads nodded. The man who was chewing tobacco spit loudly into the tin can, then spoke for the first time.

"We'll have to wear Union uniforms, ya know." There was general consternation at this. Ben jumped to his feet again.

"Union uniforms? Are you kidding me?" He looked at the men around him. "I can't believe you guys are even considering this!"

"We're as unhappy as you are, Ben," Captain Matthews said. "Just shut up and give us a few minutes to think."

There was silence as each man balanced the distasteful prospect of wearing a Union uniform with the alternative of the gallows. Ben, who had stayed on his feet, couldn't contain himself long.

"Oh, come on, you guys! How can you even think about this?"

Captain Matthews spoke again. "Ben, how many kids you got at home?"

"Three," Ben said. "Why?"

"Well, if you hang, who's going to feed them?"

Ben didn't reply.

"If we hang," Matthews said to the whole group, "we leave our families with nothing. They're sure not gonna get a pension from the Confederate Army, because there ain't no more Confederate Army. And if you think about it, that means there ain't no more Union Army, either. Like it or not, there's just the United States Army. And we're soldiers."

Several men murmured quietly. Ben said nothing. One of his buddies tugged at his arm and nodded at him to sit down.

"Well, I'll have to admit I'm all for westward expansion," said Lieutenant Watkins. "I was too young to join the Forty-Niners, but ever since then I've been itchin' to see California. Before the war broke out, I was thinking about moving my family out there. And Custer's right: We can't take our families out there until the savages have been taken care of."

Matthews looked around the group, reading each man's face and waiting for any additional comments. Then he turned to the guards at the door.

"Tell General Custer we've made our decision."

Fourteen

ANNOUNCEMENT

THREE YEARS AFTER THE WAR, on May 16, 1868, President Andrew Johnson escaped conviction in his impeachment trial by a single vote. The Radical Republicans had failed in their attempt to punish him for his leniency toward the South. The nation was abuzz with the news, so no one noticed a small article that appeared on the back pages of some of the major newspapers that day. It said the 1860 census figures had been adjusted to correct inaccuracies caused by the difficulty of conducting the census in Southern states on the verge of seceding. Cooperation with census takers in the South had been minimal from the beginning, the article said, and once Lincoln was elected in early November, hostility toward the federal government made it unsafe for census takers to complete their work. As a result, the Census Office had been forced to estimate some population figures. Only now could accurate counts be taken and the original estimates corrected. For example, the article said, the number of slaves had been overestimated in some Southern states. A state-by-state breakdown was provided. Those who took the time to tally the figures learned that almost 300,000 slaves from the original estimates could not be found. But few people bothered to add up the results, and the revised figures were never challenged. They remain the official figures to this day.

Fifteen

BACK TO 1924

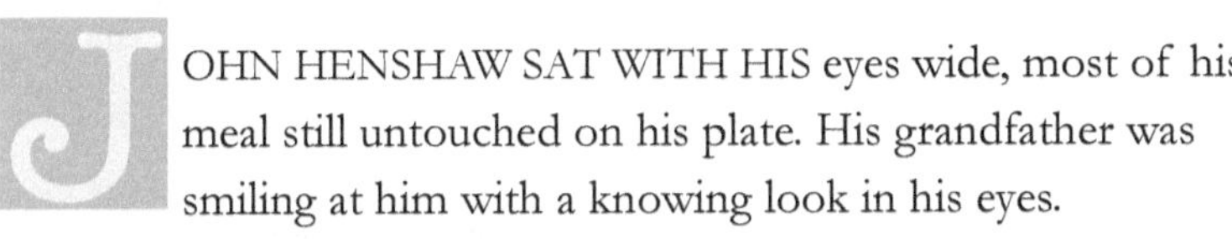

OHN HENSHAW SAT WITH HIS eyes wide, most of his meal still untouched on his plate. His grandfather was smiling at him with a knowing look in his eyes.

"Grandpa, is that story true?"

"Yep. Every word of it. I told you it was shocking."

John shook his head in sympathy. "And you've been carrying that with you all these years? How do you handle the guilt?"

Thomas looked slightly surprised by the question. John was immediately sorry he had phrased it the way he did, but before he could correct himself, his grandfather answered.

"Well, like I said, I'm not proud of what we did. It was horrible, and I take comfort in the fact that we weren't able to take it further. But you have to look at it in context. The war was horrible for everyone, with hundreds of thousands killed and maimed. Death was all around us. It was kill or be killed. Widows and the handicapped were part of our daily lives for decades afterward. And I've walked with a limp for sixty years because they tried to kill me. I can't begin to describe the pain I was in while lying in that hospital, and I'm lucky I kept my leg. So I guess the horror of what we did to the slaves is overshadowed in my mind by the horror of what the Yankees did to us, their own countrymen."

"I understand," John said.

"It's easy to sit in our comfortable homes years later and romanticize war—even we veterans do that. But it's different when it's actually happening to you—when the soldiers are marching down your street, when they've destroyed your town with cannon fire, when they've killed your friends and are trying to kill you. When you're already living in a nightmare, nightmarish things seem less nightmarish. Does that make sense?"

"Perfect sense. And I'm sorry; I didn't mean to suggest that you should feel guilty. That came out wrong."

His grandfather waved off the notion.

"Don't worry about it. My regret has never been personal. Remember, I never killed anyone or even saw anyone being killed. All I did was clerical work, and I was just following orders. Besides, my C. O. was hanged and the camp guards were killed, so there was a measure of justice meted out."

"Yes, but what about the soldiers in the execution squads, the death riders? They got away with it, didn't they?"

Thomas smiled and shook his head. "You're forgetting who they followed. These were the men who were with Custer at Little Big Horn."

John's eyes grew large again. "Wow," he said, shaking his head. "How ironic."

"Anyway, I'll always be convinced that the actions of the North forced us to do what we did. But the people causing the turmoil today don't have that excuse. They're not faced with a military necessity, but they're killing people anyway. If they hear about what we did, maybe they'll see how horrible their own actions are. That's why I want to tell my story. And it has to be told now."

"Why now?"

"Because the way we're treating the Negro is just part of something bigger. There's something much worse looming on the horizon. Something far more insidious."

"What do you mean?"

"You remember how my C. O. used Darwin's theory of natural selection as part of his justification for the program of elimination?"

"Yes."

"Well, he wasn't the only one to pick up on that idea. Since then, plenty of others have picked up on it, and now they're taking it to levels we never dreamed of, levels Darwin never dreamed of. Are you familiar with the so-called 'science' of eugenics?"

"Sure, it's the idea of weeding out the unfit in order to breed a stronger race. Say, I see what you're getting at there. I never thought about it before, but that's right out of Darwin."

"Yes, the term 'eugenics' was even coined by a cousin of Darwin's. Except that Darwin only talked about what happens naturally. Eugenics is man playing God. It takes Darwin's ideas and uses them to justify racial 'purification,' not through natural processes, but by any means—sterilization, abortion, euthanasia, institutionalization, segregation, lobotomies, even elimination. If you're poor, mentally feeble, disabled, a criminal, a member of the wrong ethnic group, then you need to be eliminated in the name of progress. This is as dangerous an idea as has ever existed on Earth."

"I know that several states have passed laws allowing the compulsory sterilization of criminals and people below a certain IQ."

"More than a dozen states, with several more considering them."

"Well, you'll forgive me, but I can't say I'm entirely opposed to sterilizing criminals and the mentally ill," John said. "Remember, I deal with these people every day."

His grandfather nodded. "If that's all there was to it, I wouldn't be concerned. But it's a slippery slope. Just two months ago, Virginia passed the nation's strongest eugenics law, one that requires everyone in the state to be classified as either 'white' or 'non-white.' The slightest bit of blood from a non-white ancestor makes you non-white. There's a movement to pass a federal eugenics law based on the same model."

"Hmm," John said thoughtfully. "That seems a bit extreme."

"If you'll indulge me, let's go back into the living room so I can show you a few things." As they took their dishes into the kitchen, Thomas kept talking. "I'm sure you're aware that a strict new immigration law goes into effect this month."

"Yes, and again, I can't say I disagree. We've allowed far too many immigrants in the last few decades."

"I won't argue with that. But the Johnson-Reed Act isn't just about reducing the number of immigrants; it's about restricting *who* can immigrate. It's also known as the National Origins Act, or the Asian Exclusion Act. It not only blocks almost all non-whites from immigrating, it even blocks whites who apparently aren't white enough, such as Italians, Greeks, and Poles. Between the Middle East and Eastern Europe, it keeps out most of the Jews. The largest quotas are reserved for those from Northern Europe—England, Ireland, Germany, and Scandinavia. Do you know why?"

"Sure," John said as he took his seat in the living room. "Northern Europeans are the pure white race, the Aryan race."

"Right," Thomas said, stopping at the table where he kept his publications and riffling through them again. "And you'll recall from my story that the idea of an Aryan race preceded the Civil War. Did you see William S. Hart's movie from several years ago called *The Aryan*?"

"No, but I remember D. W. Griffith's *Birth of a Nation*. They talk about saving America for the Aryan race in there."

"Right. The Aryan race is the pure race, and the further north you go in Europe, the purer it gets." As he talked, he occasionally selected a book or magazine and placed it on the table beside his chair. "The physical ideal is the blond hair and blue eyes of the Nordic race. Isn't that what you've heard?"

"Yes, that's right."

"Do you and I have blond hair and blue eyes?"

"No, of course not."

"So we're not the Aryan ideal, are we? We're not Nordic."

"Well, no, but we're still Aryan."

"Ah, but what if we weren't?"

"Well . . ."

Thomas placed one more item on the table, then limped around and dropped into his seat. He pulled a book from the stack and turned to a dog-eared page.

"One of the biggest advocates of our new immigration law is a man named Madison Grant. He's the one who really popularized the Nordic ideal in his book *The Passing of the Great Race*."

"I've heard of it."

"It was first published in 1916. Listen to what he has to say:

Mistaken regard for what are believed to be divine laws and a sentimental belief in the sanctity of human life tend to prevent both the elimination of defective infants and the sterilization of such adults as are themselves of no value to the community. The laws of nature require the obliteration of the unfit and human life is valuable only when it is of use to the community or race."

"Well, he certainly doesn't pull any punches, does he?"

"Nope. You can see it's far more than just the feeble-minded they're after. And I don't know about you, but to me 'obliteration' sounds like a lot more than restricting immigration quotas."

"It would seem so."

His grandfather picked up a magazine and opened it.

"Of course, when he says these things are required by 'the laws of nature,' he means Darwinian laws. Here's a quote from a University of Wisconsin eugenicist named Leon J. Cole, in which he makes it clear that their ideas come from Darwin:

> Instead of being natural selection, it is now conscious selection on the part of the breeder. . . . Death is the normal process of elimination in the social organism, and we might carry the figure a step further and say that in prolonging the lives of defectives we are tampering with the functioning of the social kidneys!

You see what he's saying there? He's saying that unfit people are nothing more than bodily wastes to be eliminated. The eugenicists even refer to it as 'racial hygiene.' Those of us who are not eliminated will be in the hands of 'breeders.' Their goal is to breed a master race, achieved through the same techniques used to breed animals. In fact, when the American Genetic Association was founded twenty years ago, it was originally called the American Breeders Association."

"Okay, I didn't know all this," John said.

Thomas pulled another book and several journals from his stack. "Eight years ago, a lady named Margaret Sanger opened something called a 'birth control clinic' in New York City. Then three years ago, she founded the American Birth Control League to take her ideas nationwide. The journal they publish is full of articles on eugenics, and she has personally spoken out for the sterilization of those she sees as 'unfit,' saying it would be 'the salvation of American civilization.' She refers to them as 'a dead weight of human waste' and complains that 'We are paying for, and even submitting to, the dictates of an ever-increasing, unceasingly spawning class of human beings who never should have been born at all.' And here, I'll let you read this one. This is from her book that came out four years ago."

John took the book and read aloud. "'The most merciful thing that a large family does to one of its infant members is to kill it.'" His mouth dropped open. "Did she really say that?"

"It's her book—look at the cover. Her argument is that a child doomed to grow up in poverty or other miserable circumstances would be better off if it hadn't lived at all. As if great people haven't risen from impoverished beginnings."

John just shook his head.

"Don't think she's unusual in her beliefs. Here's William Robinson in his book *Practical Eugenics*: 'From the point of view of abstract justice, and of the greatest good . . . , the best thing would be to gently chloroform these children or to give them a dose of potassium cyanide.'"

"Jesus Christ," John said involuntarily.

"Exactly," his grandfather said. "Except that Jesus and God are no longer part of it. They've been replaced by the God of Progress. These people even call themselves 'progressives,' a term they invented for themselves not long ago. Where Jesus spoke about morality and the value of the individual, the God of Progress has no moral qualms, and the individual has no value. All that matters is the advancement of the race. People who might slow this advancement are expendable. In fact, we have an absolute duty to dispose of them, because they stand in the way of our efforts to create a perfect world. Ironically, that's the same reasoning used by religious crusaders to burn non-believers at the stake."

"But they're not actually doing this stuff, are they? I mean, sterilization is one thing, but they're not really eliminating anyone."

"Depends on how you look at it. You're familiar with Dr. Harry J. Haiselden and the 'Black Stork' case, aren't you?"

"Sure, the doctor in Chicago who let a defective newborn die by withholding treatment. But he was found to be within his rights as a doctor."

"Spoken like an attorney. Now think about it as the father of two little girls. What if that baby had been Lilly or Allison? What if one of them had needed treatment at birth, but the doctor had refused to provide it, and she had died as a result? Would you agree then that he was 'within his rights'?"

———

John's face grew grave at the thought.

"After Dr. Haiselden was acquitted, he went on a speaking tour promoting the idea of euthanizing defective newborns. He even played himself in a movie dramatizing his beliefs. In one scene, he and the mother of a newborn let the child die, then watch as its little soul floats into the waiting arms of Jesus."

John shook his head again.

"Haiselden stated that 'death is the great and lasting disinfectant,' and he's not just being metaphorical. Eugenicists believe that people with defective strains are quite literally 'viruses' infecting the human race. Such people are not really humans; they're parasites that can be eliminated at will. And Haiselden's actions in Chicago are apparently not an exception to the rule. When he was being questioned by his medical board, he said that defective babies are regularly euthanized around the country. He also said that institutions for the feebleminded and diseased routinely withhold care, letting patients die as a way of weeding out the weak. I've got a quote here that's appropriate."

He withdrew yet another book.

"It's from Charles Davenport, the real head of the eugenics movement in America. He said, 'One may even view with satisfaction the high death rate in an institution for low grade feeble-minded, while one regards as a national disaster the loss of . . . the infant child of exceptional parents.' A 'national disaster.' You see what he's saying there? You exist for the state, for the race, not for yourself."

"I didn't know about all this," John repeated, his voice flat.

"Well, 'all this' wouldn't be such a concern if these were just extremists mouthing off, but it goes far beyond that. When the movement started in England after the Civil War, it gained the endorsement of luminaries like H. G. Wells and George Bernard Shaw. America, which has always valued the individual's will to survive and thrive, took to it naturally. Republicans like Teddy Roosevelt and Democrats like Woodrow Wilson believed in it, and Alexander Graham Bell wrote articles on it. We're now the world leader in eugenics. Our laws are being studied by other countries.

"Eugenical research efforts are well funded by groups like the Carnegie and Rockefeller foundations. John Harvey Kellogg founded the Race Betterment Foundation in Battle Creek, Michigan, using his cereal fortune. Ivy League colleges are conducting research and teaching courses in eugenics, and high school textbooks teach it. With funding and support like that, there's no telling how far this movement will go. And just a few months ago, something happened that really put the icing on the cake."

"What's that?"

"You asked me if they're actually eliminating people, and I showed you how they're eliminating defective newborns and sick people by withholding care. That's still passive euthanasia, but you can tell from the quotations I've just read that many of the leaders of the movement want to take the next step. When that time comes, their preferred method for eliminating undesirables is the lethal chamber, the kind used to put down dogs and cats. And you know what happened in Nevada in February, don't you?"

"Sure, the first person executed in a gas chamber."

"Exactly. So you see why my story needs to be told now. Strict immigration laws based on race, going into effect this month. The strictest sterilization law in the nation passed two months ago. The first execution by gas chamber three months ago. Public calls for eliminating the unfit through active euthanasia. All the various factors are aligning themselves for the possibility of doing the same thing we tried to do to the slaves. And that's just half of it."

"There's more?"

"There's another blade to the scissors. Luckily," Thomas said with a smile, "this one doesn't take as long to explain."

"Thank God," John said jokingly. They both chuckled.

"I'll make this quick. Seven years ago, the Russian government was overthrown by a communist revolution, but it didn't fully succeed. A civil war erupted that lasted years and killed millions. The last of the counter-revolutionaries finally surrendered last year. The communists claim this was a 'people's revolution,' but if the people were really behind it, why would millions of them die to prevent it from succeeding?"

"Good question."

"Just four months ago, Vladimir Lenin died. We don't know yet who will take his place, but it's pretty clear that whoever it is will be a hard-liner. Do you know what communist Russia has to do with Darwinism?"

"Not a clue," his grandson said.

"Marx and Engels said that history has been nothing but a series of class struggles. They said that capitalism would eventually—and quite naturally—give way to socialism, then to full-blown communism, a collective society in which people produce according to their abilities and take only what they need. In other words, Marx and Engels believed that society would naturally evolve"—he drew the word out to emphasize it—"from a lower stage to a higher stage. They believed human nature would evolve"—again he drew the word out—"from a selfish, greedy state to a higher, more enlightened state."

"I gotcha," his grandson said. "It's Darwinism applied to politics, to society."

"Exactly. There's even a name for it. It's called Social Darwinism. While the eugenicists have been misapplying Darwinism under the guise of the natural sciences, others have been misapplying it in the social sciences. Where the eugenicists focus on the evolution of the race, the communists focus on the evolution of society, the evolution of the state. Both groups claim to believe in evolution, but both groups seem to think evolution needs to be helped along. And of course they've appointed themselves to do so. I doubt Darwin would have approved of either."

"I never realized that communism was based on Darwinism."

"Actually, *The Communist Manifesto* was written before *The Origin of Species*, but Marx was happy to note that Darwinism supported his ideas. At Marx's funeral, Engels said—I think I have this right—'Just as Darwin discovered the law of evolution in organic nature, so did Marx discover the law of evolution in human history.'"

John nodded. "But like you said, it's not really evolution if it has to be helped along."

"Exactly. And what does that mean in practice? It means that once again, Progress has become our God. Except now it's not the advancement of the race that renders the individual expendable, it's the advancement of the state. This Soviet Union is brand new, but it's already declared that all property belongs to the state. Crops are confiscated and distributed by the state. The state decides where people will work and what they will do.

Dissent is punished harshly. All in the name of establishing a so-called 'people's republic.' Do you see how contradictory that is? It's amazing how people can be so blind."

"It sure is," John agreed, nodding again.

"Okay, I know you're ready for me to wrap this up, so here it is: On the one hand you have Social Darwinism, which allows the state to enslave its own people in the name of progress. Then you have eugenics, which justifies eliminating people in the name of progress. Now, think about what would happen if someone were to combine the two."

His grandson thought for a moment, then shook his head and let out a low whistle.

"I would hate to imagine. It wouldn't be pretty, that's for sure."

"It would be unlike anything the world has ever seen. If this isn't stopped, someone is going to use Darwinism as their excuse for wiping out entire populations, entire races. They're going to do what we tried to do during the Civil War, but they're going to succeed. You see, our only problem was that we didn't have the means. Think about trying to do the same thing with the weapons available today—aeroplanes, bombs, machine guns, gas chambers. You could wipe out millions, all because they're of 'inferior stock.' I'm telling you, if someone doesn't do something to prevent it, there's going to be a holocaust."

Sixteen

THE EVILS OF THE WORLD

AT HOME THAT EVENING, JOHN'S daughters didn't notice the extra tenderness in his eyes when he looked at them, or that the hugs he gave them were longer than usual. His wife, on the other hand, was delighted when he told her he would be cutting back on his hours at work. After they went to bed, he lay awake in the darkness, thinking about all the things his grandfather had talked about. He had been so busy with his career and family that he had hardly paid attention to the turmoil going on in the world around him.

Dozing off, he was troubled by flickering images of a bloody past, an angry present, and a fearful future. He dreamed he saw his wife screaming in despair as stern-faced social workers took away their daughters because they were somehow deemed "unfit" by the State. He saw soldiers coming to their door to take him and his wife to work on a huge collective farm, to live out their lives as slaves to a so-called 'people's republic.' He saw himself in a small Southern town, but in a society where blacks were in the majority. He was being strung up in the town square for whistling at a black woman, his protests of innocence ignored, the people below jeering at him as he was strangled by the rope.

He awoke with a start, sweating profusely. He slipped out of bed and went into the bathroom to splash cold water on his face.

After his head had cleared, he peeped into his daughters' room to check on them. Their angelic faces caused him to tarry in the doorway. Their lives were so innocent now, their world so protected. He hated the idea that they would someday have to learn about the evils of the world.

And what evils! His daughters were physically fine, but what if they hadn't been? Would the doctors have simply let them die there in the hospital? This was happening right then, in America, and there were people who wanted it to happen more often. He and his wife had worked hard to create a safe and secure home for themselves and their daughters—would the government confiscate their property in the name of making everyone 'equal'? They were doing that to people in Russia this very night. And this very night, in America, there might be a black man being lynched without a trial. The things he had dreamed were real.

Most people don't take the time to really learn about these things, or to really think them through. Most people hear ideas that sound good and adopt them without seriously considering their implications. He had been like most people.

As his grandfather said, it's easy to dismiss these things when they're not happening to you. It's easy to hear ideas for improving the world, perhaps even support them, without thinking about the suffering they would cause others. After all, when we envision these solutions, we never picture ourselves having to suffer for them. We see ourselves as directing these solutions, or at least being in the group that does. We see ourselves as the saviors of mankind. It's everyone else who must bear the burden of change. It's everyone else who must change their way of thinking to conform to ours.

Calling yourself "progressive" suggests that your views represent progress, but who gave you the authority to decide what does and does not represent progress? Meanwhile, people on the other side claim to be speaking for God Himself, and who gave them the right to do that? Both sides have found a way to declare themselves the guardians of Truth, so they feel no need to question their own beliefs or justify them to others. They are free to ignore opposing viewpoints, free to impose their beliefs on everyone else. If only the two sides could see how alike they are in this regard.

What is it about human nature, he wondered, that makes us think we have all the answers? What makes us think we have the right to impose our solutions on everyone else? Why is it so easy to see people as abstractions, and abstract theories as real? How do we so easily convince ourselves that the world could be made perfect, and that all we have to do to achieve perfection is change this law, keep that person from voting, or eliminate that group?

There's a reason for this, he thought. We're all frustrated by the state of the world, but we don't know how to fix it. Bringing about real and lasting change is difficult, if not impossible. So we look for scapegoats. Why? Because it's hard to solve problems, but it's easy to attack people.

To the communists and the socialists, the scapegoats are the rich and powerful. To the eugenicists, the scapegoats are the poor, the slow, the defective, and the members of undesirable ethnic groups. To the political parties, the scapegoats are those with opposing views. The Protestants and Catholics blame each other, and they both blame the Jews. Races claim their happiness is blocked by other races; nations by other nations.

If you can convince yourself that someone else is the cause of our problems or stands in the way of solving our problems, then you have a target for your anger. You have someone to feel superior to, someone to hate. You don't have to actually work to make the world better. You don't even need a workable plan, or a realistic vision. You just need someone to blame.

And everyone does it—religious and non-religious, liberal and conservative, North and South, black and white, government officials and revolutionaries. They all think they're right, and anyone who disagrees with them is either selfish, greedy, lazy, power hungry, treasonous, devious, subversive, hateful, or simply stupid. Why take part in productive, rational debate when you can simply assign evil motives to your opponents and attack them accordingly?

They all use the same rhetoric, even as they decry the rhetoric of the opposing side. They attack the lies and scandals of the other side while ignoring the lies and scandals of their own. They jump on the slightest mistake of an opponent, blowing it all out of proportion, then ignore their own major failings. They call for a vote when the majority is on their side, and when it's not, they declare the masses to be 'misled' and try to impose their will through other means—parliamentary tricks, lawsuits and court orders, riots and demonstrations, intimidation, violence, and the guns of soldiers.

After a while, John headed back to bed, shaking his head over the lunacy of these silly creatures called human beings. Human nature evolving? Not by a long shot, he thought. If anything, it's getting worse.

Seventeen

THE ARTICLE

"ON THE CONFEDERACY'S ATTEMPT TO Eradicate the Negro Race,' by Thomas C. Henshaw." Thomas scanned down the neatly typed manuscript, pleased with the result. It was forty-five pages long, broken into three equal sections in case a magazine or newspaper wanted to serialize it.

"Tell your secretary she's an excellent typist," he told his grandson. "And your fancy new dictating machine certainly made things easier."

"Yes, the modern world does have its advantages," John said. "Now the challenge is to get it published. I've spoken with several people who know about these things, and they've given me some good advice. We'll start with the top national magazines and go down the line from there. If that doesn't work, we'll post it to the newswire services. That way, every newspaper and magazine editor will see it."

"I'll leave all that to you. And any money it makes is yours to keep."

"Well, thanks, but that won't be necessary. We'll send it off as soon as you've proofed it one last time." He put on his coat. "Just make sure you're willing to stand behind everything you say in there. And think about whether there might be people still living who would be hurt or upset by what you've said. We wouldn't want to be hit with a libel suit."

As soon as John left, Thomas settled into his chair to read through his article. He liked his opening:

> Three score and four years ago, our fathers collided in a conflagration that nearly tore our country apart, but that ended up saving it instead. Now we are struggling with the legacy of that terrible time, with racial tensions that are a direct result of the way the war and its aftermath were managed, or mismanaged. Our country is still being torn apart, and I believe the worst is yet to come. To explain what I mean, I must begin at the beginning, with my own story as a young soldier fighting for the Confederacy.

He went on to tell the story exactly as it happened, starting with McFall's presentation that warm spring morning in Richmond and ending with his execution. He included all the things they had wanted to do—the development of a network of processing camps, the use of blast furnaces to dispose of the bodies—as a way of emphasizing what someone could do with modern tools and adequate resources. He summarized McFall's speech at the gallows, ending with his final warning: "I predict that this country will be dealing with racial issues one hundred years in the future, or longer."

"Here we are sixty years later," Thomas concluded, "and his prediction is coming true. The reasons are not hard to discern."

The second installment of the article explored those reasons:

> Just as Colonel McFall predicted, the North freed four million people without an adequate plan for providing them with a livelihood, lifting them up out of ignorance, or protecting them during the process. At the same time, the Yankees treated Southern whites like conquered foreigners, even though the entire premise of the war had been that the South couldn't leave the union. They occupied us, imposed harsh penalties on us, and allowed scalawags and carpetbaggers to take over our governments and loot our treasuries. Just as my boss predicted, they disenfranchised the whites and elected their own puppets—including newly freed, illiterate slaves—to our legislatures. For us, the world was turned upside down. It was like living in a nightmare, and it was done purely out of revenge.
>
> Why does this matter to us today? Because the backlash against the North's treatment of the South under Reconstruction led directly to the formation of the Ku Klux Klan and the first lynchings. It led to the imposition of Jim Crow laws when Reconstruction ended. It led to the poll taxes and literacy tests that are still being used to keep blacks from voting. It led to today's vagrancy laws and peonage system, which allow blacks to be arrested for virtually no reason and forced to work off their fines on chain

gangs, on farms, and in factories. In short, it led to today's racial injustices, and to the racial tension that results from them.

I wonder how many young people today have even heard of the Ironclad Oath. This was an oath the North wanted to require of all Southerners before we could vote after the Civil War. People taking the oath had to swear they had not taken part in the rebellion or given aid and comfort to those who had. Obviously, almost no Southerner could honestly swear to that. It was a clear and blatant attempt to keep white Southerners from voting and, by extension, from being elected.

And how many people today remember that Congress refused to seat the duly elected representatives of the Southern states following the Civil War, thus overturning the votes of millions of Southerners? They even passed the Fourteenth Amendment prohibiting those who had taken part in the rebellion from holding any state or federal office. Again, this was a clear and blatant attempt to disqualify those in the South with leadership credentials, disenfranchise Southern voters, and elect their own puppets.

Later, when Southern whites regained power and tried to keep blacks from voting, *they were only doing what had been done to them under Reconstruction!*

We're not the ones who came up with the idea of disenfranchising voters; *it was the North that practiced it first!* Of course, as my boss predicted, today's history books omit that little inconvenient truth.

Likewise, when the Southern states introduced Jim Crow laws, they were merely emulating practices common in the North and in the territories. From colonial days until after the Civil War, there were places in the North where free blacks couldn't vote, couldn't own land, couldn't sue whites. There were laws stating that blacks who travelled had to carry passes, could only stay in a town for a certain length of time, or had to register and pay a bond. Blacks were confined to ghettos in Boston as early as the 1760s, and many towns had exclusion laws that prohibited blacks from living there at all. So did the so-called "free-soil" territories. The North established the precedent for Jim Crow, but you won't read about it in today's history books.

After the Civil War, blacks were left vulnerable to continued injustices by the complete failure of the North to provide them with adequate support and protection during the transition phase. The Freed-men's Bureau was funded for a whopping seven years, then disbanded. And let's not forget why Reconstruction ended when it did—it ended as a political deal to secure Southern support for the election of Rutherford B. Hayes. So much for the "principles" on which the North fought the Civil War.

With no plan in place for securing a livelihood for blacks, four million people were left to wander the back roads of the South, looking for a place to fit into a society that had no room for them. The result in the agrarian South was the development of the sharecropping system, a form of quasi-slavery that's still going strong today. Those who went north looking for factory jobs were herded into ghettos, where they still live today. All of this has led to the racial tensions we're experiencing throughout our nation sixty years later.

If you think I'm placing too much blame on the North for today's racial situation, let me point out that the active racial hatred we see in America today didn't exist in the antebellum South. Under slavery, there was no reason to hate the Negro, because he was already subjugated. Remember, we thought of blacks as property, and you don't go around hating your property. The active hatred of white against black existed in the North first. In the South, it didn't begin until Reconstruction, when blacks became puppets of the North as well as competition for food and jobs. That hatred continues today in all parts of the country, and for the same reasons. Blacks are not the only ethnic group in America looked down upon by whites, but they are the most visible because of their skin color, and therefore the subject of the greatest hatred. Exactly as Colonel McFall predicted.

I am not one of those who believe the Negroes were "better off" under slavery, but I believe I'm justified in saying that the North has not left them better off than they were under slavery. Those who say that blacks were "happier" under slavery do so with some justice, not because slavery was in any way good, but because the conditions imposed upon blacks today are so miserable.

The shame of it is, it didn't have to be this way.

If the liberation of the slaves had been handled properly, America could rightfully claim its place as the citadel of liberty and equality it originally claimed to be. After all, America did not introduce slavery to our hemisphere. The first African slaves were brought here hundreds of years before America existed, and they were brought here by the Spanish. Slavery was being practiced before the British colonies were even formed, much less America, so America, as a nation, cannot logically be blamed for it. The only thing we might blame ourselves for is not ending it sooner, but let's look at what might have happened had we tried to do so:

The Founding Fathers were forced to accept slavery in order to form the union. In fact, eight of the original thirteen states—a majority—were slave-holding states. Had they not joined the United States, the Confederate States of America would probably have been formed shortly after the United States. Therefore, to say that the Founding Fathers should not have allowed slavery into the union is to wish for two separate countries, precisely what the South wanted when it seceded. And because a separate Southern nation could have done as it pleased, the South might still be practicing slavery today.

Although the Founding Fathers from the non-slave-holding colonies were forced to accept slavery as a compromise, they secured a clause in the Constitution allowing the importation of new slaves to be outlawed after twenty years. And that's exactly what they did. Congress outlawed the importation of new slaves effective January 1, 1808, the very first day they were allowed to do so under the Constitution. Even before that, they prohibited slavery in the Northwest Territory in 1787, and in 1794 they passed the Slave Trade Act, which prohibited any American ship from participating in the slave trade. These actions angered the South and helped pave the way for the Civil War, but that's just the point. The United States government did everything it could, as early as it could, to curtail slavery, even risking civil war, which eventually came to pass.

In 1865, the practice of slavery was ended altogether, at a terrible cost, and doing so came perilously close to splitting the nation. Clearly, any stronger attempt to end slavery sooner would have destroyed America. Again, doing so would have given the Confederate states their own nation, which would have allowed slavery to continue.

It seems to me that, under the circumstances, America, as a nation, did its best to end slavery as quickly as possible. Having inherited the problem of slavery, America did its best to live up to its founding principles. It was so aggressive in doing so that it nearly split itself in half, and when that time came, hundreds of thousands of white men risked and gave their lives to hold it together. And they continued to fight and die even after Lincoln's Emancipation Proclamation made the war about slavery at least as much as it was about preserving the union.

After the Civil War, Americans of African descent had cause to be the most grateful people in the history of the world. After all, what other country has gone to war with itself in order to free its own slaves? Only in America did hundreds of thousands of white men die so that black men could live free.

Had things been handled properly after the Civil War, the freed slaves and their progeny would have the right to hold their heads high as a special people, a unique example of people who were freed through the sacrifice of others. Had things been handled properly, the African in America would have cause to love this country more than anyone.

Instead, we have given him cause to be angry and fearful. We have made him a citizen but withheld from him the rights of citizenship. We have left him a stranger in a strange land, a man without a country. We have left him in a situation more dangerous and precarious than slavery itself.

And why? Because the most idealistic among us— those who demanded an immediate end to slavery— couldn't be bothered with the implications of their demands. Because those with the best of intentions grew bored with their own handiwork, leaving the people they wanted to help worse off in some ways than they had been before. The Republicans, having won the military surrender of the South, stuck up a "Mission Accomplished" banner and did their best to ignore the sectarian violence that has rocked this nation ever since.

humanity closer to its destiny. It's all scientific—Darwin said so!

In reality, of course, Darwinism supports none of this. Darwin only reported what happens in nature, without man's interference, and the changes he talked about happen gradually, over millions of years. Darwinism is about adaptation to external environments, and environments can change at any time and in different ways, wiping out advanced species as easily as others. Darwinism is about change, not progress. It is an observation about how species live and die, not a blueprint for the perfection of human society.

Any use of evolutionary theory to try to shape the world is a misuse of Darwinism. Any use of evolutionary theory to try to shape the world to our own personal vision is a path to tyranny. It is not tyranny imposed by a human dictator who might someday be overthrown, but tyranny imposed by an impersonal State, the only guiding principle of which is the Idea of Progress. This tyrant doesn't just imprison or execute those who displease it; this tyrant makes all people the property of the State, utilizing or eliminating them as it sees fit, all for the sake of Progress.

And who decides what Progress is? Ah, that's the tyranny.

Thomas closed his article with a moral appeal. But in keeping with his goal of shocking people into examining their own actions, be began with what sounded like a justification for the program of elimination:

> On what grounds can you condemn our attempt to eliminate the slaves? They were our property, to do with as we pleased. They were potential enemy combatants, making their elimination a military necessity. No one involved in the program has ever been found guilty in a court of law. On what grounds can you condemn us?
>
> On what grounds can you condemn the Confederacy? Northerners call us traitors to this day, but if this is true, why was no Confederate leader ever brought to trial for treason? Jefferson Davis was charged with treason and kept in federal prison for two years, then the charges were dropped and he was released. Why? The reason is obvious: During those two years, while preparing for Jefferson's trial, the Yankee lawyers realized they couldn't build a case that would hold up in court.
>
> A trial for treason would have to begin with a ruling on whether the Constitution created a permanent union. Since the Constitution says nothing to that effect, they knew they ran the risk of a court decision upholding the right of states to secede!

To this day, there is nothing in the law or the Constitution that prohibits a state from leaving the union. To this day, there is only one reason why you can't secede from the United States: If you try to leave, the federal government will send troops to your state and start killing people until you surrender. That is the only thing that prevented secession in the Civil War, and it is the only thing that prevents secession today. You will stay because they say so, not because the law is on their side.

From a legal standpoint, the South stands unconvicted and uncondemned for its attempt to secede from the United States. From a legal standpoint, we stand unconvicted and uncondemned for our attempt to eliminate the slaves. No matter how you feel about what we did, you cannot condemn us on legal grounds.

You can condemn us only if there is a higher law than the law of man.

The people of the South have always been a God-fearing people. After our land was laid waste by war, we couldn't understand why God had forsaken us. If our cause was righteous, why did God allow us to lose, and to lose so terribly? And how could our cause not be righteous when we had the law on our side?

Perhaps we were being taught the difference between man's law and God's law.

As Colonel McFall pointed out, the Southern states did not appeal to states' rights in their secession proclamations. They appealed instead to our inalienable rights as human beings, as set forth in the Declaration of Independence. The problem with this is obvious. We were appealing to our individual right to freedom while simultaneously holding other human beings in bondage. We may have been right legally, but we were wrong morally. The principles to which we appealed may have been noble, but the practice we were perpetuating was evil, so God abandoned us.

And where is God today? Where is morality? Not with those committing racial violence, even if they do carry the sign of the cross. Not in the eugenics programs, and not in the communist movement. Both these groups openly reject God. They have to, because Progress is their god. And when Progress is your god, people are expendable. In fact, people are property in their eyes every bit as much as the slaves were property in our eyes.

Just as we did with slavery, these groups have convinced themselves that an evil is a good. And just as it was with us, the results will be tragic.

I've told you my story to show you what such thinking can lead to. I urge my fellow Americans to take a few minutes from your stock portfolios and your jazz records and your moving picture shows to reflect on the injustice that still prevails in the land of the free and the home of the brave. Look around you, and take these things seriously, for the world is creating monsters.

Eighteen

THE AFTERMATH

"THEY ALL THINK IT'S FICTION," John said, dropping another batch of rejection letters on the table beside his grandfather's chair. "Every single one of them. No one believes it."

Thomas Henshaw showed no emotion. It had been apparent for some time that his story wasn't going to get published. Not even the Hearst papers would touch it. One reason was a letter-writing campaign by the Ku Klux Klan, which denounced the article as a "vile lie perpetuated by anti-American forces" for the purpose of "promoting internal strife while smearing our nation's reputation abroad." At the same time, urban black newspapers denounced the article as "white supremacist propaganda" and "a lynch mob's fantasy tale" that promoted violence toward blacks. Notably, none of the groups denouncing the article actually published it so that others could decide for themselves.

"So I united the races after all," Thomas said dryly. "I united them in their shared hatred of me. Now some moron who's never even read my article will probably come put a bullet through my window."

"Let's hope not," John said.

"And how can I hurt America's reputation abroad when the article hasn't even been published?"

"That's the other thing I had to tell you. I just found out it was picked up by some of the radical rags in Europe—the tabloids put out by the communists and socialists. Of course, they're only printing it to make America look bad."

Now Thomas Henshaw's face showed distaste. "I didn't mean to make America look bad. And I certainly didn't mean to help the communists or socialists."

"I know, Grandpa."

"Is there some way we can stop them from printing it?"

"I'm afraid not. Putting it out on the newswire gives anyone permission to publish it. But I wouldn't worry about those groups. Nobody reads their stuff. Besides, except for Russia, every communist and socialist uprising in Europe has been put down. With the economy so good, they can't get much of a foothold."

Thomas sighed. "Well, I tried. If people won't listen, there's nothing I can do. I was just trying to help. I'm sorry you went to all that trouble for nothing."

"Oh, don't worry about that, Grandpa. And besides, don't give up yet. We knew this was going to be shocking to people; maybe they just need a little time to absorb it. It's certainly getting publicity, so it could still have an impact. We just have to get it in front of the right people."

Meanwhile, on the other side of the Atlantic, another man with a limp hurried through the cobblestone streets of a central European town. One hand grasped a bundle of newspapers by his side, while the other held his up-turned collar tight around his neck against the frigid February wind. When he saw the warm glow of the beer hall ahead, he smiled, and not just because of the cold. He knew that he was about to be the center of attention, and this played to his ambitious nature. He had purposefully arrived late so he could make a grand entrance. He climbed the steps to the private room above, peeked in to make sure there was nothing that would detract attention from him, then swept into the room flourishing the papers above his head.

"Gentlemen! I bring you the news!" The buzz of excitement was exactly as he had hoped. Every conversation stopped and every eye turned to him as he distributed copies. He had joined the Socialist Party less than a year before, but he had snared a position of leadership by offering to restart the party newspaper.

"That's right, gentlemen, the first copy of our newspaper, reborn. Featuring an essay by our esteemed leader, appropriately titled 'A New Beginning.'"

"Wunderbar," said the author of that essay, who was seated at the head of the table. He took his copy eagerly and looked at it with undisguised pride. The newspaper's editor continued to hand out copies, talking as he did to keep the focus on himself.

"The head of the National Socialists meets with the Premier of Bavaria and convinces him to remove the restrictions on our party," he said, summarizing the headline story. "It truly is a new beginning for our party, and for the cause of socialism."

"Yes," said their leader. "This is the beginning. We will rebuild, and nothing will stop us this time."

"I've also included the article by the American," said the editor, omitting the fact that he was publishing only the first of three parts. "It starts on page four."

"Ah, yes," said their leader, flipping to the article and reading the title out loud. "'On the Confederacy's Attempt to Eradicate the Negro Race,' by a Mister Thomas Henshaw. Clearly the leaders of the Confederacy understood the implications of Darwinism before anyone else."

His followers nodded in agreement.

"Perhaps that is why the Americans have led the world in implementing measures to improve the human race. They, more than any other country, have had the courage to reject the false morality of individual rights for the sake of racial hygiene. They, more than any other country, have instituted programs to preserve the Aryan race. I refer to the American programs in my book, which is almost ready for publication. In it, I call for expanding such measures in Europe."

Again the men nodded in agreement. Their leader folded the newspaper back to Thomas's article and laid it on the table.

"Of course, Herr Henshaw and I have a difference of opinion," he said. This caught the attention of his followers, as he knew it would. "When he talks about America's effort to eliminate an inferior race, he condemns it. He means this article to be a confession, a warning. But I . . . ?"

His followers leaned in, anxious to hear his opinion.

"I say he has shown us the way. We are already dedicated to the cause of racial purification; now he has shown us how to implement it. This," he said, patting the article, "this is our blueprint."

He smiled, a knowing gleam in his eye. His followers smiled too, as they realized his meaning. They chuckled, then one by one began to laugh. Beer steins were raised and backs were slapped as the group merrily endorsed their leader's idea.

"Yes, it is our blueprint," they said. "We will use it as our blueprint."

One of the men raised his beer stein high and cried out, "Jawohl, Herr Hitler!"

"Jawohl, Herr Hitler," repeated every man in the group. And the celebration went on into the night.

--- THE END ---

AFTERWORDS

IS THIS STORY TRUE?

By Douglas Cupples, Ph.D.
Instructor (retired), U.S. Military History and Civil War & Reconstruction
Department of History, University of Memphis, Memphis, Tennessee

 PROGRAM OF ATTEMPTED GENOCIDE BY the South during the Civil War, as depicted in the short novel *Final Solution*, did not occur, nor was it ever considered. There are no reports that any slaves were ever killed for the purpose of preventing their liberation by Union troops. In fact, such an effort would have run counter to the Southern *casus belli*, which was independence and expansion of the slave-based cotton economy. As this book suggests, even if a rogue element had attempted to eradicate the slave population in the last year of the war, there was not the will, culture, or technology to make it possible.

Despite this, *Final Solution* is not just one more entry into the "alternative history" genre. Rather, this is fiction with a purpose. The provocative premise is really just a springboard for exploring aspects of this key period in American history that are seldom covered in school or discussed in television documentaries. The story also serves as a useful commentary on subsequent historic events, present-day social and political issues, and human nature in general.

While the program of elimination and the characters who attempt it are fictional, *Final Solution* is set against an historically accurate background, both in the events that surround its characters and in the arguments these characters put forth. For example:

- It is true that the revolutionaries in Haiti massacred the white colonists, and it is true that they justified their actions with the arguments reported by McFall to young Tommy Henshaw.

- John Brown did indeed plan a widespread massacre of white Southerners, and his plan was supported and funded by private citizens in the North. Brown was widely lionized in the Northern press, leading many in the South to abandon any hope of reconciliation between the two sides.

- The fear of slave uprisings in the South was real and widespread, and is therefore a plausible motivation as used by McFall.

- The African country of Liberia was founded by freed American slaves, hence its name. Lincoln supported colonization and made unsuccessful attempts to expatriate free blacks to other countries.

- In a reversal of the generally accepted view of the debate on states' rights, Northern states nullified and ignored the Fugitive Slave Act designed to uphold Article Four of the Constitution. At one point, President Millard Fillmore threatened to send federal troops to Vermont to uphold the law. The Southern proclamations of secession cited this failure to follow federal law as an invalidation of the contract that created America.

- When Lincoln instituted the draft, there were riots in New York that turned into mob attacks and the lynching of blacks.

- Historians agree that the harsh policies of Reconstruction created a backlash that contributed to the formation of the original Ku Klux Klan, the imposition of Jim Crow, and the widespread use of lynch law.

- The last federal troops were withdrawn from the South by Rutherford B. Hayes soon after he took office, reportedly as part of a deal for securing Southern support during the election.

- In 1910, Baltimore tried to confine blacks to designated areas, and many Southern cities followed suit. Racial zoning was declared unconstitutional by the U. S. Supreme Court in 1917 in *Buchanan v. Warley*.

- The "Red Summer" race riots of 1919 were motivated primarily by job competition following World War I. It is true that white thugs in Tulsa dropped incendiary bombs on black neighborhoods from an old WWI surplus biplane.

From this historically accurate setting, the authors have drawn insights and pointed out details that will be new and striking to many readers. For example:

- Many readers will not have considered the fact that America, as a nation, inherited the problem of slavery, nor would they be aware that Congress did all it could, as early as it could, to limit and then end the practice.

- Many will be unaware that the precedent for Jim Crow was set prior to the Civil War in Northern cities and states and in the territories, which routinely limited the rights of free blacks or attempted to exclude them altogether.

- How many will have thought about the fact that America is the only country ever to go to war with itself in order to free its own slaves?

- Who wouldn't be disturbed by the realization that our government, while in the very process of freeing the slaves and granting them citizenship, was simultaneously wiping out America's native population, using the same argument of racial inferiority that had been used to justify slavery? (And using some of the same soldiers, too. The blue uniforms of the U. S. Cavalry as it rides to the rescue in old Western movies were Union uniforms worn by soldiers sent west after the Civil War.)

As these examples suggest, *Final Solution* does an excellent job of showing the complexity of the issues surrounding the Civil War and the Jim Crow era, a complexity that can only be fully appreciated after in-depth study. McFall's speeches are not meant by the authors to justify the Confederate cause, but to show us just how simplistic and stereotyped our views of this period tend to be. By exposing the inconsistencies and hypocrisies of both sides in this particular conflict, and by doing so in an historically accurate manner, the authors demonstrate that history, like life itself, is not so simple.

An example of this complexity can be seen in the debate between McFall and Dickinson regarding the use of the word "traitor." Northerners referred to the Confederates as traitors before, during, and after the Civil War, and that term is still used in history textbooks today. But is that term appropriate for separatists who do not attempt to overthrow a government or betray it to a foreign power? If it is, why don't we refer to the Founding Fathers as traitors against England? What about the Baltic states that rebelled against the Soviet Union? Did the ill-fated uprising of the Kurds against Saddam Hussein make them traitors against Iraq? (Hussein thought so, which is why he gassed entire villages.) Is the connection between rebellion and treason purely one of perspective? Interesting questions to ponder, and a good example of the complexity of life in general and politics in particular.

There are a few instances in *Final Solution* where the authors have made slight alterations to the historical setting. The scenes with Custer and Hitler are obviously fictional, and Custer did not go west so quickly after the war. But more important are the anachronisms purposefully included by the authors to make the story serve as a mirror to today's world. By cleverly inserting modern events and phrases into a story set in the 19th and early 20th centuries, the authors signal to us that they are commenting on our own societal tensions and polarized politics. They are also showing us that the more things change, the more they stay the same. For example:

- It's hard to argue with the criticism of the North for ending slavery without a workable plan for protecting and providing for the freed slaves, and the implied comparison to George W. Bush's "Mission Accomplished" invasion of

Iraq is sure to draw a smile. Meanwhile, the fictional "No Blood for Cotton" slogan parallels the real "No Blood for Oil" used by opponents of the Iraqi War.

- Because of the South's practice of slavery, it's easy for us to dismiss the arguments for secession that were made at the time. However, as this story shows, these arguments centered on questions about the appropriate role of our federal government, and that is certainly a topic still being hotly debated today.

- McFall's appeal to the separation of church and state would be unlikely at that point in history, but it is true that the abolitionist movement was centered in the church, as was the Civil Rights movement of the 1960s. Would those who today argue for a strict separation have denied those movements their right to advocate for social change?

- While the fictional attempt at Holocaust-type genocide in this story failed, similar efforts came terrifyingly close to succeeding in the next century, and not just in Nazi Germany. Genocide and ethnic cleansing have been a horrific legacy of 20th-century warfare. Even though the elimination of a race or culture is counter to the objectives of war among nation states (the Holocaust drained significant military resources from the Nazi war effort), it was aggressively pursued in both World Wars and has been pursued in multiple places since—Cambodia, Rwanda, the Balkans. This misguided idea remains with us today, and it will be with us tomorrow, so it is worthy of both our study and our attention.

Through the anachronistic placement of state-sponsored civilian genocide in the Civil War era, *Final Solution* shows us that the philosophical underpinnings of the Holocaust go back further than we think. It shows us how these ideas continue to affect us in ways we don't even realize. Most importantly, it shows us that the evils of the world are always with us, hiding just under the surface, waiting for the right moment to burst forth yet again.

Final Solution provides an intriguing look at some of the ideas and actions that have shaped the country—and the world—we live in today. Hopefully, it will inspire us to do a better job of shaping the world of tomorrow.

ON THE ORIGIN OF OUR STORY

By Dale A. Berryhill and Kevin P. Henry
Co-authors, Final Solution

ON JANUARY 20, 1942, OFFICERS of the Nazi regime met in the Berlin suburb of Wannsee to organize the logistics of what they referred to as the "final solution of the Jewish question." We know it as the Holocaust. The Wannsee Conference was dramatized in a 1984 German-language film, then again in the 2001 English-language film *Conspiracy*, starring Kenneth Branagh. Both movies draw their dramatic force from the Nazi leadership's use of carefully crafted, seemingly logical, but ultimately diabolical arguments to justify the unjustifiable.

In the opening chapters of our novella *Final Solution*, Lieutenant Colonel Troy McFall of the Confederate Army uses the same type of arguments for the same purpose. But why would we superimpose the events of one war over another?

The American Civil War and World War II were fought seventy-four years apart, on different continents, for totally different reasons and under totally different circumstances. They did, however, have one thing in common: In both wars, a large group of innocent civilians were caught in the middle, civilians who were set apart by their ethnicity and viewed by their oppressors as subhuman.

There is even an historical event that ties the two together: Before the Holocaust, Hitler attempted to relocate the European Jews to Africa, just as Lincoln and others had tried to relocate America's blacks prior to the Civil War. As with Lincoln's efforts, Hitler's Madagascar Plan fell apart because of logistical challenges.

What would have happened, we wondered, had the South victimized its civilian ethnic group the way the Nazis did theirs? Since we know they did not, this would have been a question of only passing interest were it not for one other coincidence: The Holocaust was the result of a belief in racial superiority based on Darwinism, and Darwin published his theory of natural selection just before the Civil War. The American Confederacy had no goals for ethnic cleansing and did not base its belief in racial superiority on Darwinism, but chronologically speaking, it *could* have, and that made the idea more intriguing.

When further research showed that the terms "Aryan" and "master race" were already in use—and, most importantly, that the term "master race" now associated with Nazism had actually been coined in the slaveholding South—we were compelled to pursue the idea.

With this tantalizing premise in mind, it was a simple matter to envision the Wannsee Conference taking place during the Civil War. All we had to do was revise the leadership's diabolical arguments to fit the time and place. When we did, we were taken aback by the results. Where the Nazis had only racial hatred as their motivation, and where the Holocaust distracted from the Reich's military goal of world domination, McFall's arguments actually made sense from a military standpoint. We leave it to the reader to decide which is more chilling.

The only thing missing was the method. The poison gases used by the Nazis had not been invented in the 1860s, and even barbed wire was just being patented as the Civil War ended. Then we learned about the *Einsatzgruppen* regiments.

When German troops entered Russia in 1941, they were accompanied by four regiments spread out along the front lines from north to south. Operating independently of the military command, the sole purpose of these mobile killing units was to eliminate the Jews and other "undesirable" civilian populations in the conquered territory. While the concentration camps and gas chambers were still being built back in Poland, these troops rounded up Jews, took them away from population centers, forced them to dig their own graves, and shot them. According to Raul Hilberg's *The Destruction of the European Jews*, of the six million Jews killed in the Holocaust, more than a million were eliminated by these mobile execution squads. Genocide by rifle was both plausible and historically accurate, so the "death riders" in our novel took center stage.

With these elements in place, we knew we had the makings of an intriguing and controversial story. What we didn't know was just how deeply interwoven were the lines of thought that ran through these two wars and up to the world of today. Nor did we realize how deeply profound were the lessons that could be learned by those able to discern them.

CHARLES DARWIN AND THE IDEA OF PROGRESS

By Dale A. Berryhill and Kevin P. Henry
Co-authors, Final Solution

MERICA WAS BORN DURING A time of rapid scientific, technological, and societal advances. The Industrial Revolution was reshaping the physical world, while the Age of Enlightenment placed a new emphasis on rational thought, the scientific process, and the rights of man. As this unprecedented change continued and accelerated, people began to assume that progress was natural, inevitable, and linear. They began to assume that man would eventually solve all of his problems. They began to believe in what scholars now call the Idea of Progress.

In 1819, when America was only thirty years old, a young college graduate named Horace Mann gave the valedictorian speech at Brown University. The theme of his talk was "the progressive character of the human race." In 1837, he began laying the foundation for America's public education system, his stated goal being the creation of an egalitarian society.

In 1848, Marx and Engels published the *Manifesto of the Communist Party* in Europe. They spoke of the "progressive historical development" that would naturally culminate in an egalitarian society. Declaring this outcome to be "inevitable," they insisted that human nature had evolved to the point that people would voluntarily take part in a collectivist society.

In 1851, England's Prince Albert hosted the "Great Exhibition of the Works of Industry of all Nations," commonly referred to as the Crystal Palace Exhibition. A celebration of all that capitalism had brought to the world, it stood in stark contrast to the railings of the communists except for its belief in an unlimited future. As Prince Albert put it, "We are living at a period of most wonderful transition, which tends rapidly to accomplish that great end to which, indeed, all history points—the realization of the unity of mankind."

Clearly, the Idea of Progress was in the air before Charles Darwin came along.

When Darwin published his theory of natural selection in 1859, he seemed to be providing a scientific basis for the Idea of Progress to a world that was primed for it. Darwin himself was influenced by the Idea of Progress, ending *On the Origin of Species* by declaring that, "as natural selection works solely by and for the good of each being, all corporeal and mental endowments will tend to progress toward perfection."

Unfortunately, such an optimistic sentiment finds no support in Darwin's own scientific theories, which state that organisms change through adaptation to specific environments. What constitutes "perfection" in an organism depends on where that organism is, and what it needs to do to survive and thrive. When environments change, advanced species can be eliminated as easily as lesser species. An asteroid wiped out the dinosaurs; another asteroid might wipe out humanity. If mankind were to kill itself off through nuclear war or global warming, the cockroach might well emerge as the dominant species on Earth. Under Darwinism, if there is any "progress" among organisms, it is a mere accidental byproduct of natural selection, with no guarantee of permanence.

None of that mattered to an age enamored with the Idea of Progress. The very fact that Darwin was only talking about biological changes in organisms was quickly forgotten, as the belief took hold that everything evolves, and that evolution always represents progress. How nice it would be if this were true.

The Price of Progress

George Washington was still in his first term as president when Eli Whitney invented the cotton gin. Large quantities of cotton could now be processed quickly, significantly reducing the cost of clothing and other textile products for people around the world. By the 1830s, America was the world's top producer of cotton, and the export of cotton surpassed the value of all other American exports combined.

But it came at a price. When America was founded, there were eight slave states and around 700,000 African slaves in the country. Thanks largely to the increased demand for cotton, by 1860 there were fifteen slave states and around four million slaves. The money generated by cotton made it possible for the South to fund an extended war, while overseas dependence on Southern cotton not only kept Europe neutral, it even gave hope to the Confederacy that England or France would intercede on its behalf. The invention of the cotton gin clothed the world, but it also expanded, extended, and prolonged slavery in America. In doing so, it helped bring about the Civil War.

The trade-offs of technological progress were clear from the early days of the Industrial Revolution, when new factories created hellish working conditions and ecological disasters. Today, we've learned that technological progress almost always comes with a price, from pollution to the dangers of nuclear power. Belief in an unlimited future must now be balanced by the very real possibility that we may destroy ourselves and even our planet before we get there.

We've also learned that human and societal progress is harder to obtain and maintain than are scientific and technological advances. Despite a century and a half of effort, we haven't attained the egalitarian society envisioned by Mann, Marx, and Engels, much less the "unity of mankind" envisioned by Prince Albert. Even slavery continues to be practiced in parts of the world.

Today, the Idea of Progress has been tempered with realism, if not cynicism. But in the decades between the Civil War and World War II, it permeated the thinking of the Western world in a way no new philosophy had since the introduction of Christianity.

The Progressive Era

After all, who could argue against the Idea of Progress in the age of Jules Verne and H. G. Wells, with its visions of space travel, videophones, and personal jet packs? Who could argue in the face of rapid-fire inventions such as the electric light bulb, the telephone, the phonograph, motion pictures, the automobile, and the airplane? And if technology was advancing, surely society would, too.

An American reform movement that began in the 1880s promoted what was referred to as "Progressive" education. This expanded into a wider Progressive movement that brought about important reforms in machine politics, labor law, trust busting, women's suffrage, and the conservation of natural resources. Even the hundred-year-old temperance movement was able to make prohibition the law of the land. Historians now refer to the period between the 1890s and the 1920s as the Progressive Era.

It was widely understood that the Progressive movement found its genesis in evolutionary theory. Theodore Roosevelt, America's first Progressive president, illustrated this when he addressed the faculty of Oxford University in 1910. According to biographer Edmund Morris, Roosevelt spoke about "the development of higher life forms" and the factors "that determined which species should flourish or disappear." He then applied these factors "to the evolution of societies." Neither he nor his audience questioned the validity of applying biological laws to human society. As historian David H. Burton puts it, "The social milieu in which Roosevelt moved and with which he came to share convictions was permeated with Darwinism."

Faith in societal progress had become so strong that World War I was quite seriously referred to as "the war to end all wars." Progressive president Woodrow Wilson expressed hope that the war would "make the world safe for democracy" and envisioned a world united in peace under his League of Nations. In the wake of the war, communist and socialist parties throughout the world gained support by promising "people's republics" and "workers' paradises." As it turned out, of course, the 20th century was by far the bloodiest and most repressive in human history, and those who promised the most ended up committing the worst atrocities.

By the end of the Progressive Era, the reformers who led it were calling themselves "progressives." Why didn't they simply refer to themselves as reformers? Because under the Idea of Progress, reforms are no longer just a way of righting wrongs or ensuring justice. They also represent progress toward a better world, if not a perfect world, and they are evaluated not just on moral grounds, but on how well they fit the future vision of the reformers. The importance of that distinction was soon to be demonstrated with horrifying clarity.

The Progressive Era, along with the continuing scientific and technological advances of the early 20th century, lifted the belief in progress to its zenith. The theme of the 1933 Chicago World's Fair was "A Century of Progress" despite the fact that it took place in the middle of the worst worldwide economic downturn of the modern era. The theme of the 1939 New York World's Fair was "Building the World of Tomorrow" despite the fact that the Great Depression had not ended and the bloodiest war in the history of the world had already begun. In fact, World War II was itself started out of a misguided belief in the Idea of Progress.

Hitler's Dream

You see, Adolf Hitler believed in the Idea of Progress more than anyone. While war raged around him, he spent hours with architect Albert Speer designing his own City of Tomorrow, a remake of Berlin called "Germania" that would serve as the capital of the world. Like Prince Albert, Hitler wanted to unite mankind, albeit under Nazi rule. Hitler didn't start World War II out of mere personal ambition, but to establish nirvana, a perfect socialist world ruled by a pure Aryan race. And how was this perfect world to be achieved? Through the Darwinian principal of natural selection applied on a racial level.

In *Mein Kampf,* published in 1925, Hitler paraphrased Darwin by referring to "nature's will to breed life as a whole towards a higher level." He paraphrased Darwin again in describing how this evolution takes place: "The fight for daily bread makes all those succumb who are weak, sickly, and less determined. . . . But the fight is always a means for the promotion of the specie's health and force of resistance, and thus a cause for its development towards a higher level."

Hitler accepted the Darwinian concept of "survival of the fittest" not just as a law of nature, but as a means for bringing about human progress through human effort. "The man who misjudges and disdains the laws of race," he wrote, "prevents the victorious march of the best race and with it also the presumption for all human progress." He called for "a new State" based on this "racial idea," declaring that "the paramount purpose of the State is to preserve and improve the race; for this is an indispensable condition of all progress in human civilization."

Yes, Hitler believed in the Idea of Progress. He combined a belief in the perfectibility of the race with a belief in the perfectibility of the state, and the results were catastrophic. But he didn't come up with these ideas on his own.

The Eugenics Movement

In 1883, the year after Darwin died, his cousin Francis Galton coined the term "eugenics" for his research into the application of Darwinian principles to human beings. Galton took the name of his new scientific discipline from the Greek word for "well born." Eugenics isn't merely the study of heredity; it is the proactive effort to improve the quality of the human species through "proper" breeding. By the turn of the century, Galton's ideas had spread throughout Europe and moved across the Atlantic. Science was building better mechanical devices; now it was going to build better people, literally.

Like the Idea of Progress itself, eugenics became almost universally accepted. For example, French author Albert Robida's 1890 science fiction novel *The 20th Century, The Electrical Life* predicted modern biological warfare two decades before it was practiced and suggested it would have one beneficial outcome: Whereas bullets could kill anyone, biological weapons would weed out the weak through natural selection. Those strong enough to survive would be best suited for propagating the species.

By the end of World War I, eugenics had evolved into its fullest form, complete with compulsory sterilization laws, race-based immigration laws, and terms like "racial hygiene." According to the eugenicists, it isn't just race, physical disabilities, and mental deficiencies that are inherited. Our genes also determine behavior such as criminal activity and welfare dependency. The 1914 Model Eugenical Sterilization Law, which served as the template for several state laws, included the blind, deaf, and homeless as groups to be forcibly sterilized.

America led the world in eugenics, as symbolized by the "Better Baby" and "Fitter Family" contests held at state fairs. In 1927, the U. S. Supreme Court upheld the forced sterilization of the mentally challenged "in order to prevent our being swamped with incompetence" by "those who already sap the strength of the State." This ruling prompted the re-release of the 1918 pro-euthanasia movie *The Black Stork* under the title *Are You Fit to Marry?* The movie continued to circulate right up until the atrocities of the Holocaust first became known.

Eugenics provided a scientific justification for racial segregation, anti-miscegenation laws, and white supremacy. Interestingly, though, the Ku Klux Klan did not associate itself with eugenics, preferring to base its belief in racial superiority on Divine Providence rather than Darwinism. In contrast, American eugenics leaders thought of themselves as part of the Progressive movement and referred to themselves as progressives. They envisioned a man-made utopian future, to be achieved by discarding what Madison Grant called the "mistaken regard for what are believed to be divine laws and a sentimental belief in the sanctity of human life." Their efforts were opposed by the church in much the same way that abortion is opposed by the church today. Their efforts also helped lay the groundwork for the Holocaust.

America and the Holocaust

In 1903, the American Breeder's Association was founded with the stated goal of determining the laws of inheritance in plants and animals (including humans) and applying these laws to increase the value of living things (including humans). The breeding of humans was discussed side-by-side with the breeding of horses, and association members such as Alexander Graham Bell followed in Galton's footsteps by analyzing who should and should not be allowed to marry. Adolph Hitler echoed these ideas when he looked forward to "a nobler era, in which men will no longer pay exclusive attention to breeding and rearing pedigree dogs and horses and cats, but will endeavor to improve the breed of the human race itself."

The connection between American eugenics and the Nazi Holocaust was not just philosophical. In his landmark 2003 book *War Against the Weak* and other writings, author and researcher Edwin Black shows that:

- Eugenics research in America and Germany was funded by the Carnegie and Rockefeller Foundations and the Harriman railroad fortune before and during the Nazi regime. Eugenics officials from the two countries visited, corresponded, and attended conferences together on a regular basis.

- California's forced sterilization program and America's 1914 Model Eugenical Sterilization Law were specifically cited by the Nazis as models for their own sterilization program, a precursor to the Holocaust.

- Hitler personally wrote to American eugenics leaders such as Madison Grant, calling Grant's 1919 book *The Passing of the Great Race* "my Bible."

- In his 1925 book *Mein Kampf,* Hitler praised America for leading the world in implementing "commonsense" eugenical measures, adding that the Americans "have begun to introduce principles similar to those on which we wish to ground the People's State."

- The idea of an Aryan/Nordic master race was part of the American and international eugenics movement long before it was adopted by Nazi Germany, as was the whispered idea of eliminating "defectives" by poison gas.

- In 1936, Harry H. Laughlin, head of America's Eugenics Record Office, was awarded an honorary doctorate from Heidelberg University for his work in "the science of racial cleansing." The ceremony was scheduled to coincide with the second anniversary of Hitler's purge of Jewish faculty from the university.

- The eugenics-inspired racial quotas set by the Immigration Act of 1924 prevented many European Jews from seeking shelter from the Holocaust in America, and similar quotas in Europe blocked their escape to other countries.

- At the Nuremberg trials, Nazi war criminals cited the U. S. Supreme Court's ruling on forced sterilization as part of their defense.

As you can see, Hitler did not originate the ideas that led to the Holocaust. The Holocaust was not an aberration that sprang from the mind of a single madman, but the culmination of threads of thought that pre-dated the Civil War. Hitler simply implemented what was already being talked about openly, by men and women of standing, in America and elsewhere.

The Nazi's use of Darwinism to justify their actions was explicit. For example, the official minutes of the Wannsee Conference include this passage (emphasis added):

> Able-bodied Jews, separated according to sex, will be taken in large work columns to these areas for work on roads, in the course of which action doubtless a large portion will be eliminated by *natural causes*.

> The possible final remnant will, since it will undoubt-
> edly consist of the most resistant portion, have to
> be treated accordingly, because it is the product of
> *natural selection* and would, if released, act as the seed
> of a new Jewish revival.

In that last phrase, we see the same justification for murder used by Jean-Jacques Dessalines in Haiti a century before, but now with a pseudo-scientific basis that renders moral concerns moot. To understand the difference this makes, one must realize that Jewish ghettos did not start in Nazi-occupied Poland, but had existed for centuries throughout Europe. Anti-Semitism had been practiced ever since the rise of Christianity, primarily, of course, as a form of religious persecution. The Jews suffered under discriminatory laws and were often the victims of violence, but like the treatment of African Americans by the Ku Klux Klan, these actions were designed to punish Jews and keep them "in their place," not to eliminate them as a race.

That changed with Darwin and Galton. Darwinism replaced religion with race, then eugenics declared race to be the key to human progress, if not the key to the very health and survival of the human species. Suddenly the Jews (and others) were no longer heretics to be converted or an annoyance to be contained, but a biological threat to be eliminated.

The difference was fundamental. Jews had been persecuted for centuries for what they believed; now they were slaughtered because of who they were. Other countries had herded Jews into ghettos; the Nazis emptied theirs. In one fell swoop, the Idea of Progress and the eugenics movement it spawned took more lives than all of history's religious wars, crusades, and martyrdoms combined.

As Edwin Black points out, the eugenics movement continued long after the horrors of the Holocaust were known. America's race-based immigration laws weren't repealed until 1965 and anti-miscegenation laws weren't ruled unconstitutional until 1967. The last legal forced sterilization in the United States was performed in 1981. By that time, some sixty thousand Americans had been forcibly sterilized, most without any court order and without having committed any crime.

One has to wonder how far the eugenics movement might have gone had the Holocaust not so brutally demonstrated where it could lead. America's forced sterilizations, along with the withholding of care from defective infants and the chronically ill, did not require messy public displays of armed soldiers or the relocation of undesirable populations. The eugenics movement in America claimed its victims one by one, out of the public eye, in trusted institutions, with government approval, when the victims were helpless and voiceless. Had these activities not been stopped, who knows what kind of world we might be living in today, and what type of control doctors and unelected bureaucrats might have over our bodies and our lives? Perhaps, by discrediting and putting the eugenics movement to an end, the victims of the Holocaust did not die entirely in vain.

Afterword: Four

A NATION DIVIDED

By Dale A. Berryhill and Kevin P. Henry
Co-authors, Final Solution

THE CIVIL WAR WAS NOT inevitable. Slaveholding states joined in voting to end the importation of new slaves after 1808, and the abolitionist movement remained small and marginalized into the 1840s. Even in the North, abolitionists were derided as rabble-rousers and their printing presses were destroyed by mobs. Congress agreed in the early 1840s to automatically table any petition to end slavery. Then, in a ten-year period beginning with the Fugitive Slave Act of 1850, events such as Bleeding Kansas, Dred Scott, and John Brown's raid generated reactions and counter-reactions that polarized the nation and led rapidly to disunion and war.

David M. Potter, in his excellent book *The Impending Crisis, 1848–1861*, traces the escalating rhetoric that both created and chronicled the increasing polarization. Southerners, for example, went from defending slavery as a constitutional right and the proper relationship between the races to declaring it as a positive good for the enslaved. Northerners went from denouncing slavery as evil to denouncing Southerners themselves as morally depraved sadists who deserved to be slaughtered and their cities torched.

Potter's review of the rise in animosity prior to the Civil War shows that both sides:

- stopped communicating with each other,

- stereotyped and demonized their opponents,

- ignored the complexity of the situation and started talking in clichés and slogans,

- listened to information sources that supported their views while closing their minds to facts that might moderate their position,

- used increasingly vehement rhetoric in lieu of reasonable, rational debate, and,

- started skirting or ignoring the law and the democratic process.

Sound familiar? Surely this list could be applied to the state of public discourse in America today.

By Any Means Necessary

The Civil War took place because Americans began to hold two opposing worldviews that could not be reconciled. The same seems to be true today. But, as our story points out, the liberals of yesteryear held positions and used methods that are today identified with conservatives, and vice versa. As our story also points out, the two sides switched methods whenever it helped their cause, just as they do today.

For example, when the Fugitive Slave Act of 1850 was enacted, Northerners passed laws and issued court rulings attempting to nullify federal law, while Southerners welcomed this expansion of federal power. When the *Dred Scott* decision was handed down, it was the liberal reformers in the North who

declared that states do not have to abide by the rulings of the
U. S. Supreme Court, while the conservative South cheered what
was undoubtedly the greatest example of judicial activism in our
nation's history. Soon after, of course, the South was defying
federal authority and the North was insisting on obedience to it.

Fast forward to the 2000 presidential election. America was
so evenly divided that the margin in the popular vote was only
one-half of one percent. It all came down to Florida. The
Florida Supreme Court, made up entirely of Democratic
appointees, unanimously ordered extra time for a manual recount
in contested counties. Democrats cheered this party-line ruling,
while Republicans decried it as politically motivated. The U. S.
Supreme Court stepped in and, in another straight party-line vote,
the conservative majority stopped the recount, thereby settling
the election for George W. Bush. Needless to say, the Republicans
who had decried the party-line vote in the Florida Supreme Court
welcomed the party-line vote in the U. S. Supreme Court, while
Democrats did exactly the opposite.

As David M. Potter puts it, the events leading to the Civil
War "offered a telling demonstration that the attitude of various
groups in a society toward upholding the law is in direct proportion to their approval or disapproval of the law which is to be
upheld." The events occurring in our country right now also
demonstrate this, as the two sides cry out against government
intrusion in the areas where they don't want it while demanding
it in the areas where they do. Meanwhile, the shouts of defiance
from both sides grow louder each year.

The one principle that both sides consistently adhered
to in the Civil War era, and the one principle that both sides

consistently adhere to today, is their unwavering belief that it is okay to use the power of the government to impose their worldview on America. As in the Civil War era, the majority of Americans do not support the more radical views of either side, and as in the Civil War era, the radicals on both sides couldn't care less.

A Nation Divided

America today is a nation divided. In fact, we believe America is more polarized now than at any time since the Civil War. The real purpose of our novel is to shine a light on this division and to sound a warning about the damage it can do. That's why we included in our story modern phrases calling attention to the similarities between then and now.

Are we suggesting that America may be headed toward another Civil War? Not in the traditional military sense. But we are suggesting that our nation is headed toward a crisis of disunity. And we believe this crisis could prove to be more dangerous than the Civil War, both for the country and for its people.

To understand why we say this, think back to the Great Depression of the 1930s, America's last major domestic crisis of a sustained nature. Even though the Great Depression affected almost everyone, the social structure remained essentially intact for more than a decade. Why? Because in those days, there were shared values concerning proper behavior.

Compare this to the 1960s, when our shared values were openly questioned for the first time. Rather than an orderly and unified effort to address the issues of the day, America fragmented into factions—hawk vs. dove, old vs. young, hippie vs. establishment, feminist vs. chauvinist, white vs. black. The result? Protests and riots that were answered by police and even military action in our streets. The loss of shared values and the polarization of society led to disunity and violence.

And today? Today in America, shared values no longer exist, and polarization is endemic. Should things fall apart today—economically or otherwise—there is no longer a moral consensus that will hold society together until things get better. If we were to be hit by a major and long-lasting downturn today, it would be every man for himself.

If America reaches the tipping point as it did in 1860, we will not have an armed conflict between two armies meeting on the battlefield. We will not have another civil war. What we will have is anarchy, and anarchy is always followed by tyranny.

It is in this context that we hope our book will be read, pondered, and discussed. Like our character Thomas Henshaw, it is our hope that telling this story might shock some people into re-examining their opinions and educating themselves further on these issues. It is our hope that Americans might cool their divisive rhetoric, turn away from polarizing politicians, and ignore sensationalistic journalism that focuses on our differences instead of our commonalities. It is our hope that both sides might acknowledge the validity of positions that differ from their own and respect the right of others to be part of the discussion. Only in this way can we heal the divisions in our society.

Most of all, it is our hope that people will pay attention to the lesson dramatized in this book, a lesson that history has taught us repeatedly: There are no final solutions, and those who seek to impose them usually do more harm than good.

FURTHER READING

THE CIVIL WAR

To understand the complex historical background of the
American Civil War, we recommend David M. Potter's
The Impending Crisis, 1848–1861, which the *New York Times*
calls "the best single-volume survey of the political events
that led to secession and war."
The Ordinances of Secession and the Declarations of Causes
adopted by the Confederate states are available online.
The text to William J. Grayson's 1855 poem "The Hireling and the
Slave," in which he apparently coined the term "master race,"
is available online.
Also available online is information about American slave revolts,
John Brown's raid, black exclusion laws, efforts to recolonize
freed slaves to Africa and other countries, the New York draft
riots, and other historical events referenced in this book.

THE EUGENICS MOVEMENT

To learn the horrors of the American eugenics movement, and
to see how the international eugenics movement led to the
Holocaust, read Edwin Black's exhaustively researched 2003
book *War Against the Weak: Eugenics and America's Campaign to
Create a Master Race*.

DARWINISM

To see how the misapplication of evolutionary ideas has shaped the world in which we live, watch episode eight of the 1985 BBC Series *The Day The Universe Changed*, which is available online. In this series, science historian James Burke gives an entertaining overview of how Darwinism led to the eugenics movement and simultaneously provided a foundation (or at least a justification) for fascism, communism, and robber-baron capitalism.

NAZI GERMANY

Conspiracy, the 2001 dramatization of the Wannsee Conference starring Kenneth Branagh, is available online.

The minutes of the Wannsee Conference (known as the Wannsee Protocol) and background information are available for reading online.

For more specific insight into the mindset of Hitler that led to his rise to power, World War II, and the Holocaust, we highly recommend Robert G. L. Waite's *The Psychotic God: Adolf Hitler*. Among other things, this "psychological biography" shows how Germany, as a nation and as a society, was particularly primed for the eugenics message, and for the militarism that provided the structure for its implementation.

Basic information about the *Einsatzgruppen* regiments is available online. For a more in-depth look at these regiments and the administrative logistics of the Holocaust, see Raul Hilberg's book *The Destruction of the European Jews*.

www.ingramcontent.com/pod-product-compliance
Lightning Source LLC
Chambersburg PA
CBHW020629110726
47899CB00002B/708